Manly

Maureen O'Leary Wanket

Giant Squid Books ◆ Washington, DC

ISBN: 0692286837
ISBN-13: 9780692286838

Cover art by Jillian Blazek

A project of Giant Squid Books:
Founded by Readers to Support Writers

Giant
Squid
Books

This is for Jim.

Table of Contents

1

Hefty Boy

If I trace back everything that happened
during the summer it all changed, it started the
day I was trying on jeans in the Hefty Boys.
The store where I buy clothes at is too polite to
have a Fat Kid department. Somebody
thought it was better to call it Hefty Boys.
Hefty Boys pants are sized by how many
letters X they can fit by the letter L. You start
off with the size L, which is pretty skinny for a
Hefty Boy. Then it goes up to XL, XXL, and so
on. It doesn't go past 4 X's. By then I guess
the people who make clothes figure the Hefty
Boy has problems they can't help him with.
There was a guy who was on one of
Grandma's talk shows who lay in bed all day

hollering for his mom to bring him food. He was so fat they couldn't even get him into the studio. The cameramen had to go to his house. A couple weeks later they did a follow up show and it turns out that guy died and firemen had to take his body out the window with a crane.

That fat man on the TV show was on my mind when I pulled up a pair of XL jeans in the dressing room of the Hefty Boys. XL was the size I usually got but I should have known better because my old pants were too tight. I folded in my stomach like a big taco and pulled up the zipper. I didn't even try the button. I stood there for a minute to see how stupid my fat looked. I jumped up and down to see it jiggle around.

I needed XXL at least. The thing was, I didn't feel like telling Grandma to go get a bigger size. She wouldn't care or be mad. It was just that the guy on TV needed to be loaded out on a *crane*. Maybe I would keep getting more and more Extra Large until nothing ever fit me and I couldn't get out of bed.

Grandma got past the attendant and knocked on the dressing room door.

"You all right in there, Matty?"

"I'm fine Grandma," I said.

"You sure?"

"Yeah. I'll be right out."

My forehead was sweaty and my stomach hurt. I unzipped. Carefully.

My legs must have expanded or else the jeans got tighter because I could not pull them off me. I took a deep breath and sucked everything in as much as I could. I pulled so hard I was shaking. Still nothing. They would not come down.

Another kid went into the stall next to me. No matter how fast I tried to go it didn't make a difference. The jeans weren't coming off.

The seams dug into my legs like razors. I couldn't catch my breath. I had a crazy thought that these were jeans of evil and that they meant to kill me.

"Grandma," I called. The boy in the other stall snorted.

"Matty. I'm right here," she said. I unlatched the door so that I could hide behind it.

"I'm stuck," I said.

She put down her purse and ordered me to stand still. She hooked her thumbs in the belt loops and crouched down and pulled. The jeans moved an inch. She farted a little bit and I thought the kid in the next stall was going to die laughing. I wished he would.

Grandma acted like she couldn't hear. She got a look in her eyes like she was going into war. She told me to lie down on the floor.

"Maybe we can just get a pair of scissors—" I suggested, but Grandma wouldn't have it.

"On the floor," she said. I had to do it. I must have lost my mind to think that Grandma would ever pay for a pair of jeans that were cut up with scissors. I tried to position my head so the kid next to us wouldn't think I was trying to look at him from underneath. Grandma bent over to grab the cuffs and then stood straight so that my feet were sticking up in the air. She pulled as hard as she could. The fabric squeezed my legs but those stupid jeans were no match against Grandma. They gave way. When she fell back the whole stall rattled like it was going to fall down.

The store worker pounded on the door, yelling that this was the BOYS DRESSING ROOM ONLY. Grandma neatly folded the jeans that tried to kill me into a big blue square and wiped her face on it. She went out and asked for the next size up.

"Go on," she said, following the worker down the aisle. "We don't have all day."

I wasn't in the mood for shopping anymore. The kid from the other stall walked past, shaking his head like I was the funniest thing he'd ever seen. I shut the door.

I didn't know what one Hefty Boy was laughing at another one for anyway.

After trying on more stuff I walked out with a couple XXL pairs that just fit. Triple X would have been more comfortable but no way was I going that far.

What happened next was even worse than getting stuck in those jeans. Grandma was standing by the register talking with Coach Grimes. My P.E. teacher. To make it worse, Coach's daughter Jessica was with them. She stared up at the Hefty Boys sign with a picture of this happy looking fat kid on it. Whoever designed the Hefty Boys department should have known better than to put it right by the door to the parking lot so people coming into the mall had to walk through. They should have put it in a corner somewhere. Better yet, underground. In a cave.

Jessica hung out with the jock types at

school. She went to the same church as me but I didn't know her well enough for it to be okay for her to see me at the Hefty Boys. If anybody at school found out they would tease me every day until I graduated or died.

I crept backwards towards the dressing rooms where I would be safe. Jessica couldn't follow me in there. It was for boys only. The guy in charge even said it. But Grandma spotted me. She waved me over. Coach Grimes nodded like he knew what I had been trying to do. He would come in after me, too. He'd pull me out before ordering ten push-ups right there on the floor.

Jessica smiled. Maybe she was laughing.

I tried to look cool, like this wasn't a nightmare.

Grandma touched the back of her afro lightly and smiled. "Look who's here, Matty," she said. "Mr. Grimes tells me that you should go out for football."

"I think we could use him on the team,"

Coach said. He was still looking at me. "Tryouts are over, but I would make an exception for your grandson, Mrs. Sullivan. We could train him for Junior Varsity. He'd make a good offensive lineman with hard work."

Coach put his hand on my shoulder and squeezed. His hand was huge and it kind of hurt.

He patted me on the back a couple times then crossed his arms in front of his chest. His muscles bulged out. There was a rumor at school that Coach lifted this kid George over his head like a barbell at a football practice. He gave me the eye like he was wondering if he could do the same to me.

I looked down at my shoes while they talked about football so he wouldn't get any big ideas. I didn't think he could lift me but I didn't want him to try it. I was having a hard enough day. Grandma was saying that she would think about signing me up for football like I wasn't standing right there to ask about it. The answer would be no and she knew it.

Jessica tapped my arm. "I'm so sick of school. Only one more day til summer," she said.

Her father's voice boomed through the whole mall. He was laughing at something my grandmother said like they were best friends all of a sudden.

"I know," I said.

"Are you doing anything fun for vacation or whatever?" she asked.

"Just hanging out. You?"

Jessica shrugged. She was wearing a tank top and her skin looked smooth. I tried to remember which sports she played. I tugged at the front of my shirt so it wouldn't stick to my chest and outline my man boobs. After what I'd just seen in the dressing room mirror I wasn't taking any chances.

"I'm helping my dad train the team over the summer," she said. "He's paying me to spot in the weight room and carry water. Stuff like that."

"That's cool," I said.

"Are you going to Mike's party tomorrow?" she asked.

"Yeah."

"Maybe I'll see you there," she said. Coach Grimes was giving my grandmother a card with his number on it. Jessica turned to wave at me as they walked away.

"What a wonderful man," Grandma said as we went to the car. "So nice that he took the time to say hello. Kyle's mother and I were friendly before she passed away, you know."

"Huh," I said. Grandma was friendly with everybody. It was hard to think of Coach Grimes as a guy named Kyle. It was hard to think of him having a mother. As a matter of fact, I didn't think Coach Grimes had ever been a kid.

"You should go out for the team. Kyle seems to think you'd be good at it."

"Yeah right," I said.

"His daughter is very pretty. Didn't you think so, Matty?"

"I don't know."

"If you weren't so hung up on that Cassie Bale, you could see that Jessica was flirting with you."

"Grandma!" I said. Luckily there was nobody near us in the parking lot. Grandma laughed even though there wasn't anything funny.

"You've been holding a torch for Cassie for too long and it's time to blow it out," she said. "Maybe you should call up Jessica Grimes. I have their phone number right here." She waved the card Coach gave her in my face.

I put on my sunglasses and walked faster. I told Grandma that I liked Cassie way back in eighth grade before I knew better than to tell her anything like that. Anyway, I could never make Grandma understand what it was between Cassie and me. I couldn't just "blow out the torch." Even if I could, Jessica would probably never like me either. That was something else I could never make Grandma understand. She thought I was the best looking guy who ever lived.

It was a million degrees outside. Grandma and I looked around right quick as she passed me the car keys. I was only fifteen and didn't even have a learner's permit yet so I wasn't exactly supposed to be driving. But Grandma didn't like driving and when Grandpa failed his DMV test when I was in seventh grade, she taught me how. I liked it. I was the only kid I knew in the freshman class who could drive a car.

Once I got behind the wheel I put the air conditioner on full blast. Grandma stopped teasing me about my love life. She got back on the subject of football.

"I think you should give the team a try. Just go for one practice," she said.

"Grandma. No."

14

She just clicked her tongue and kept on talking about how much fun it would be for her and Grandpa to sit in the stands and watch me play and wave a pom-pom at me while I ran down the field. Me, the kid she'd just had to rescue from a pair of Extra Large jeans in the boys dressing room. It didn't make sense.

It also didn't make sense that Coach Grimes even wanted me to play football. I could barely do the mile run in P.E. Plus, the man scared the crap out of me. Maybe this was his way of getting back at me for being slow in P.E. Maybe he was just trying to be nice to Grandma. Either way, Grandma could buy my clothes without me next time. If I didn't like what she picked she could bring it back. No more stupid dressing rooms in the Hefty Boys. No more going to the mall where there might be P.E. teachers and girls.

We went to the drive-thru for dinner. I passed her the food and she put it in the back seat. The whole car smelled like French fries by the time we got home.

Grandma was cheerful as she brought the shopping bags into the house. "It's settled. You're going out for football," she said.

"No way," I said. But I wasn't sure. Grandma couldn't literally *make* me go out for football. Could she?

2

The Biggest Mistake

We had to go to the drive-thru because Grandma didn't want to cook. We didn't sit in restaurants anymore because Grandpa couldn't go out too much. He was getting more and more confused. Sometimes he would be all right but other times he might get up in the middle of dinner and walk out. He did that the last time we were at Denny's, before we paid the check. The waitress got all mad because she thought we were trying to leave without paying. She almost called the police. She was too dumb to see that Grandpa didn't know what was going on and that he was crying. I thought Grandma was going to knock the waitress upside the head.

We never went to a restaurant since then.

Grandma let me get everything I liked with extra fries, the milkshake and the soda. We ate at the kitchen table because that was one of Grandma's rules. It didn't matter if we were having takeout or something she made. We always ate together at the table.

Grandpa had a patch over his right eye because the doctor took out his cataract. It was putting him in a good mood because it made him feel like a pirate. He was even cheering me up.

"Don't forget to take your medicine," Grandma said.

"Aye, matey," Grandpa said. He swallowed his pills with water. I did not know how he could take so many pills every day without choking. He never complained, though. It was like part of Grandpa knew that his dementia was hard on us too. For example, Grandma had to get our neighbor Mr. Manlow to come over whenever she needed to go anywhere with me because Grandpa wasn't safe by himself anymore. It was like he didn't want to make it worse for us by complaining over stuff like the pills.

"Scurvy knave," Grandma said. She kissed him on the head.

Sometimes I wondered what my grandparents were like when my dad was a kid. I hardly ever saw my dad. He lived a couple hours away in San Francisco and Grandma said he was busy working all the time. He was a cook in one of those restaurants on a pier, Grandma said. My mom died when I was two but my grandparents were already taking care of me by then.

My mom and dad never got married. They never even meant to have a kid. I was kind of a mistake but Grandma did not allow me or anybody else to say that. In fact the only time I ever saw Grandma get mad at my dad was when he visited us on my fourteenth birthday, when after I blew out the candles on my cake he raised his can of beer and said, "To Matty, my biggest mistake."

She never yelled at him before but she did then. I was shocked. I guess Dad was shocked too because he left the house and didn't come back. Pretty soon I was going to be sixteen and I hadn't seen him since he walked out on my fourteenth birthday.

After dinner I sat at the table for a while. I looked down at my big stomach. It was let loose in a pair of old sweatpants and a new t-shirt Grandma bought me. I had a strange feeling that I was looking down on somebody else's stomach.

I wondered what my dad would think if he saw me now. I wondered what he would say about going out for football. He never played any sports in school. Sometimes he asked me what I thought about different basketball players when he called but I never knew what to say because I didn't follow any teams.

I cleared the paper bags and wrappers off the table while my grandparents watched Jeopardy on the TV. I poured my milkshake down the sink so Grandma wouldn't notice. Even though I was not as hungry as usual it made me sad to watch it go down the drain. I sort of regretted it. I wondered if I should have saved it for later. I really loved milkshakes.

Then the sink backed up. The disposal was falling apart but Grandma said we couldn't afford a new one. Luckily I was good at fixing things. I kept an Allen wrench under the sink. It took a while but I reset it so the dirty water swirled down like it was supposed to. I wished everything could be fixed that easy.

***

After dinner, Grandma wanted me to check on Mr. Manlow. Mr. Manlow was an old guy about the same age as my grandparents and he lived next door. I pretended to forget to go over there but Grandma caught me going up to my room.

"Make sure that Mr. Manlow has everything he needs," she said. She patted me on the cheek. "It's the least we can do to thank him for keeping Grandpa company for us today."

The fences between our backyards had a gate. I knocked on the sliding glass door until Mr. Manlow showed up to let me in. Stacks of boxes lined the living room walls. It wasn't a mess or anything, but he had been living there for six months and he still wasn't all the way unpacked.

"Can't stay long, Mr. Manlow. Grandma just wants to know if you have everything you need."

The old man didn't take the hint. "You might have heard of my son." He waved me towards an open box. A gold and silver plaque rested on the top. "Do you ever play football, Matthew?"

"Grandma says I have to go right home," I said.

"Oh. Okay," he said. "Maybe some time you would like to come over and see some of my son's things."

"Some day," I said. "Goodnight, Mr. Manlow."

He held out a shaky hand. I was afraid I was going to break it but I shook it anyway. I didn't grip too hard. He always asked me to look at his son's football stuff but I never took him up on it. Mr. Manlow was okay. He let me swim in his pool over spring break. But the last thing I needed after that day was to listen to Mr. Manlow talk on and on about his son who played football. I mean, I didn't care.

Cassie called in the middle of the night. My cell phone buzzed by my head where I kept it just in case she needed me.

"What's up?" I tried to make my voice sound deeper. Whenever she called, my heart beat so fast and so hard I was surprised she couldn't hear it over the phone.

"My parents are screaming at each other," she said. "I think I heard a crash or something. I'm so scared. I'm really really scared." She was crying. I was the one she called when this happened. I was the one she could trust.

"Let's talk about something," she said, sniffing. "You going to Mike's party tomorrow? Because I got a new two-piece. Do you think Jack will be there?"

The thought of Cassie in a two-piece was spoiled as soon as she mentioned Jack. Jack was the guy she liked. He was on the varsity football team even though he was a freshman like us. I didn't know him but I didn't like him. I hated him, actually.

"I don't know if Jack's going," I said. "Why don't you ask him yourself?"

"Oh my God," she said. "Yeah right."

Somebody screamed in the background. Cassie just kept talking over it. I bet if she called Jack on the phone all he would talk about was football. Cassie knew she could always count on me. That's because I loved her. Grandma was right about that even though it wasn't any of her business.

I loved Cassie. I wanted to be her boyfriend so bad it was killing me. Some day she would have to see me as more than a friend. Sometimes I thought it could happen. There were fat guys at school with girlfriends. Maybe their girlfriends were not as hot as Cassie, but still. It didn't have to be impossible.

"Uh-huh," I said every now and then. She liked to do most of the talking. But it was okay.

Her voice was the only thing I cared about. Yeah, I was a Hefty Boy. But I was also the guy that Cassie Bale called when she was sad. That had to count for something.

"I can only see myself with someone who plays football, you know? " she said. My skin prickled all over. The room felt too hot. "The problem is that most of the players on the team think they're macks. They don't listen and they don't know how to treat girls." She sighed. "I just have a weakness for athletic guys. I can't help it."

I went to the window. It creaked as I slid it open with one hand. The night wind carried the smell of warm sidewalks and the chlorine of backyard swimming pools.

"Matty? Are you listening to me?"

"Uh-huh."

I could be on the football team if I wanted. I could make myself into Cassie's type. The thought of running around in the heat, getting yelled at by Coach Grimes and looking like an idiot made me want to die a little bit. But I could do it.

I pressed my nose against the screen to take a deep breath of fresh air. I could do it. I could go out for the team. Anything would be worth it to get Cassie.

Then the front door slammed. Grandpa's bald head flashed white beneath the wide leaves of the elm tree in our front yard. His pajamas flapped around his thin body. He headed for the street.

I opened my mouth to yell at him to stop. The front door slammed again and Grandma ran out in her bathrobe. She caught him before he stepped off the curb. The yell got stuck in my throat.

"Did you say something?" Cassie asked.

"No."

"Jack's like, not the kind of guy that settles down with one girl," she said.

"Uh-huh," I said.

My grandparents hugged each other in

the wind. For a second they looked like they belonged on the cover of one of Grandma's romance books if only they were written for old people. But then Grandpa's shoulders shook and his cries were louder than the clatter of the windblown leaves of the tree. The back of his head looked as breakable as an egg.

"Matty? You there?" Cassie asked.

"He's getting worse," I said.

"You mean Jack? Yeah I know," she said. "He's so in love with himself."

I didn't mean Jack. I was talking about Grandpa. He'd never wandered out in the middle of the night before. What if it happened again? If nobody woke up to catch him he could get lost. He could get hit by a car.

I held the phone away from my ear while Cassie kept talking. I tiptoed out of my room and listened at the top of the stairs. My grandparents were back in the house. Their bedroom door clicked shut.

"Are you there?" Cassie said.

"Yeah."

She went on talking but the great feeling I had when she first called disappeared.

Grandpa was getting worse.

3
Fatty Matty

Mr. Manlow couldn't walk as fast as his dog wanted to go so he paid me ten dollars a week to take him out in the mornings before school. Dirty Harry was a nice enough dog so I didn't mind walking him every day.

Well, I didn't exactly walk him.

Grandpa first got the idea to drive Dirty Harry on his walk back in March when it rained for five days straight. By the third day of rain Mr. Manlow said that Dirty Harry needed a walk so bad that he kept peeing on the floor and chewing up shoes. The problem was I really didn't want to go out in the storm.

Grandpa said we could try driving around the neighborhood while holding Dirty Harry's leash out the window. It wasn't as tiring as walking him ourselves so we got in the habit.

Grandpa didn't remember anything about the night before when he ran across the front lawn in his pajamas. If he did he wasn't mentioning it. Grandma had purplish circles under her eyes but she wasn't talking either.

I helped Grandpa into the car and then went through Mr. Manlow's gate to get the dog. Dirty Harry was a big long-haired German Shepard and he looked mean if you didn't know him.

"Dirty Harry," I called. "Come here, boy."

He seemed sick. He lay down on the back porch pressed up against the sliding glass door. He looked up at me with sad eyes. I felt around to see if he had a sore leg or something. There was nothing wrong with him. He was just acting like a punk for no reason.

Grandpa had on his eye patch. He was

still in a good mood about it. He took the leash through the window and I got in on the driver's side.

"How's Bob Manlow today?" Grandpa asked.

"Didn't see him," I said. Dirty Harry stayed on the sidewalk. We hooked two leashes together to make his lead extra long. On the regular route around the block he never had to go into the street.

"You should check in on him when we get back," Grandpa said. "Bob's one of the good guys."

"Sure, Grandpa," I said.

We had just enough time to take Dirty Harry around once if I was going to be on time for school. I had pushed the snooze button five times. After getting off the phone with Cassie I'd decided to get up early and actually walk the dog instead of drive him. I needed to start getting in shape if I was going to play football. But then when it came to the morning

I didn't feel like getting up. The idea of going out for the team seemed really far-fetched.

Grandpa talked to Dirty Harry through the window. The dog kept whining and acting like we were killing him by making him go for a tiny little walk. When we turned the corner and headed back towards home, he changed his mood about it. He started running and I had to speed up so that he wouldn't strangle himself. The whole operation did not go as smoothly as usual. If Cassie ever saw us drive the dog I would probably die. If anybody saw us that morning almost dragging Dirty Harry more than walking him, we would probably get arrested.

By the time we got back there was barely any time to get to school. In Mr. Manlow's backyard I gave the dog some water. He seemed all right, even though he went straight back to his place by the back door. The same old boxes were piled up by the window. Mr. Manlow must have been in bed sleeping. I was jealous of that. Next week would be summer vacation and I planned on sleeping in every day.

"How's Bob Manlow this morning?" Grandpa sat in his place on the old couch on the porch. He liked to sit there in the mornings and eat a donut and wave at people.

"He's good, Grandpa," I said. "He says to say hi."

"Bob's a good guy," he said. "And you're a good boy."

***

The teachers gave us report cards at the end of the class periods because it was the last day of school. I got a B in English and a C in everything else except Algebra. Mrs. Grant was trying to flunk me in Algebra.

Mrs. Grant looked nice when you first met her. But as soon as she started teaching she was terrible. She was too strict and she loved to get mad over nothing.

She passed out our grade reports and there was a huge F on mine. I went up to her desk.

"You gave me an F," I said.

"Sit down, Matthew," Mrs. Grant said. "You don't have permission to leave your seat."

"F for fat," this kid named George said. He was the one that Coach Grimes supposedly lifted over his head. "Fatty Matty."

It seemed like George's comment should've made me mad, but it didn't. I was so used to being called Fatty Matty that it didn't even sink in anymore. Besides, I had bigger problems. Failing Algebra meant summer school.

The bell rang and everybody rushed to go. Mrs. Grant held up her hand and everybody froze. Then she nodded and everybody unfroze. That was just like Mrs. Grant. Even though it was the last class of the last day of school, she had to let you know she was in charge.

"I didn't give you an F," she said after everybody was gone. "You earned an F."

"I got a good grade on the final," I said. "You can't do this. I'll have to take summer school."

"You *passed* the final exam, that's true." She smiled like we were talking about something good. She reminded me of a shark. "I wouldn't call a C minus on the final a good grade, however. You did fewer than half of the homework assignments all year."

"So? If I pass the tests, who cares if I do the work?" I shoved the report card into my backpack. "You can't make me come to summer school. My grandmother will come down here and talk to the principal."

"Oh, Matthew," she said. Something in her voice made me stop messing with the backpack. She looked at me real seriously. She always took everything too seriously.

"You'll either come to summer school, or you'll retake Algebra 1 in sophomore year when you should be in Geometry."

"So?"

"So, then you won't be on track to take the higher math classes you'll need to get into college."

"So?" I hoped my friends were still waiting outside. I didn't want to have to walk to Mike's pool party by myself.

"What do you mean, so?" Mrs. Grant stood up. "We're talking about your whole future here, Matthew. What kind of person are you going to be?"

It was just a stupid grade that I didn't deserve. She had to turn it into drama about my entire life.

"My Grandma will talk to the principal," I said. "Then you'll have to change my grade. I passed the final."

"See you in summer school," Mrs. Grant said. She waved me away. My mouth opened and then I closed it. I ran out before I got myself in trouble with what I wanted to say.

Grandma would stand up for me. There was no way I was going to summer school. It wasn't fair.

Mrs. Grant didn't know everything. She didn't know anything.

***

Mike and Jester were the two guys I mostly hung out with in ninth grade. They were the same guys I mostly hung out with back in junior high too. After I got out of Mrs. Grant's room they were waiting for me at the flagpole out in front. Jester's real name was Jesse but everybody called him Jester because he was crazy. Mike was the opposite of crazy. He was the shyest kid I knew.

A bunch of people from the freshman class hung around Jester and Mike. The last day of school was the only day we were popular.

Every year since we were in sixth grade, Mike's parents made him throw a big end-of-the-year party in their backyard. Mike's dad used to be in the NBA and he's pretty famous. You wouldn't have known it from looking at Mike, though. He wasn't any more athletic than me. He wasn't fat but he wasn't in real good shape either. If it were up to him he would never have a party at his house. I think his parents hoped it would help him make friends besides Jester and me. Mostly Mike just wanted to go to his room and play *Call of Duty* or watch TV.

When I got there Mike started walking towards his house like he was going to get executed, not have a party. The sun reflected off his glasses and made him look even nerdier. A bunch of kids followed us a few steps behind. Then they moved past us so that we were following *them* to Mike's house. Nobody talked to us that much.

"How's it going, Matt?" Jessica Grimes walked with us for a while. My face got hot. If she mentioned seeing me at the Hefty Boys in front of Jester he would go off on it and never stop. I just shrugged and felt relieved when she gave up trying to talk to me and went to be with her regular friends.

Cassie acted like she didn't see me yet, or that she saw me but forgot to say hello. At least Jack wasn't there. Cassie's hair was long and shiny. I wanted to pull it or something for a joke but I was afraid she'd get mad. I had to play it cooler than that.

Mike's house was at the top of a hill. It was tiring walking all that way under the hot sun. I wished that we didn't have to walk. I thought maybe next year Mike could get his parents to rent limos.

Mike's mom was already at the door with a bowl of chips. She acted real happy to see everybody, like the long line of kids were all her son's long time friends. She even acted like she was happy to see Jester and me. Usually when I came over she would let me know that Mike had homework or an appointment to go to so I couldn't stay too long. Jester sometimes she didn't let in at all. You could say that Jester's name was in the mouths of a lot of people. If you believed half of the rumors you would think he wasn't a very good person, but he was. He had a rough time with his dad and he was kind of crazy, but he was a good kid.

Their house was big. It was more like a mansion. Mike's room was pretty regular even though it was bigger than mine. But the downstairs had high ceilings and tiled floors like a museum. Everything was clean and polished and enormous. The big leather couches and wall-sized televisions made you think it was a house for giants.

Kids looked all around and I could tell they wanted to see Mike's dad. This was the only time any of them got to be in Mike's house because for the rest of the year he stuck to his two best friends, Jester and me.

Mike said people just wanted to be friends with him because of his dad. He said that Jester and me were different because he knew Jester from kindergarten. Besides that, since junior high Jester always paid for us when we went to the movies or whatever so Mike never thought that he was using him because his dad was rich. Jester's dad wasn't rich. He didn't even have a job. But Jester always had cash and he liked being the one to pay for things when we did stuff. Something about Jester always made us have a good time when he was around.

As for me, I didn't know anything about basketball and had never even heard of Mike's dad. Mike found that out when we were computer lab partners in sixth grade and we were friends ever since.

Later on, Mike sat at the edge of the pool with his feet in the water. He looked down at the soda in his hand, the sun reflecting off his eyeglasses. His mom held a tray of little hot dogs rolled up in biscuits and talked to people for him. I was too hot from walking all the way up there. I wished I could take off my shirt and jump in the pool but that was impossible. No way was I going to put my swimsuit on in front of all those people. No way was I going to take off my shirt.

Then Mike's dad came out all casual like he had fifty kids over at his pool every day. Mr. Morris had on a white shirt and aviator sunglasses and he was tall. A couple of guys went up to shake his hand and some people pretended to ignore him. While they were pretending to ignore him they started showing off on the diving board. It made me sad for Mike. He just bent over more into his soda can.

I went to where Cassie was laying on a towel. She was too cool to join the group of girls making excuses to walk past Mr. Morris in

43

their bathing suits.

"Look how dumb Stacy and them are," Cassie said when I sat down. "Like Mr. Morris is going to be into a bunch of teenage girls."

"He wouldn't be," I said. I wanted her to know that I could come over to Mike's house whenever I wanted. "Mr. Morris is really cool."

"I know." She turned over onto her back. "It's just gross what they're doing."

"Yeah," I said. Secretly I was glad that her friends were distracted by Mike's dad for a second. It was a relief that Cassie wasn't pretending not to know me. She didn't care if people saw us talking. She just hadn't had a chance to say hi before with everybody around.

On one of our phone talks Cassie said that her group of friends was lame and she didn't know why she hung out with them. But she didn't always say hi to me when she was with them in the halls at school. Sometimes she could look right at me and I'd be smiling like a big clown and then she would walk by without saying anything. But other times, like on the phone when she needed somebody to talk to, or there by the side of Mike's pool, we were cool.

I had to look away for a minute. It was impossible to just sit there and stare at Cassie in her bikini all day. Pretty soon how much I liked her would start to show. I didn't have that much control over certain parts of my body when Cassie was around.

Jester was doing a bunch of show off stunts off the diving board. He did a big flip and landed in the water flat on his stomach with a huge smack. I mean, it was loud.

Everybody stopped talking and watched as Jester bubbled to the surface and pulled himself out of the pool. His skinny white stomach was bright red.

"Freak," Cassie's friend Stacy said. A bunch of people laughed.

Jester shook out his long hair like a

sheepdog over some girls until they screamed. Mike's dad held out his hand. "You okay, Jesse?"

Jester slapped his hand like he was giving him five. He was trying to look cool but I could tell that he was hurting. I felt bad for the guy. He limped over to us.

"Dude," I said. "That was awesome." He gave me the finger.

Mike's mom saw him. "Jesse, I saw that." She said. "None of that rudeness here. You know better."

Cassie laughed at him. Jester smiled in an evil way before turning on me.

"Look at Fatty Matty," he hooted. "He's got a hard-on for Cassie."

Then he pushed me as hard as he could. I fell across Cassie like a tipped rhinoceros.

"Matty loves Cassie!" Jester yelled. Cassie was slippery from suntan oil. I couldn't find a place to put my hands as I flailed around on top of her.

"Gross!" Cassie screamed.

I put all my weight on my knee and pushed off. Cassie stood up and yanked her towel off the ground. She wrapped it around her body like I had fallen on top of her on purpose. She ran inside the house.

I didn't know what to do. Jester was already running back over to the diving board. I was crouched down on the concrete, pain shooting up my knee, staring at the empty space where Cassie had been.

I couldn't move. I was paralyzed. Maybe if I stayed totally still people would think I was a statue and stop looking at me.

"Way to go, Fatty Matty!" George said. The girls laughed like a bunch of witches. Mrs. Morris gave me a look like she was mad at me and then followed Cassie inside.

Grandma would have called it rude for me to just get up and leave without saying thank you for having me over but I didn't care. I barrelled through the house and out the front door without saying anything to anybody, not even Mike. I passed Jack on the front porch ringing the doorbell with a towel around his neck. He didn't have a shirt on and his six-pack abs peeked out from the ends of the towel.

I hated that guy.

***

It must have been five miles between my house and Mike's. I never walked it before. Grandma always brought the car and let me drive us home.

At least I didn't have to see anybody for three months. Maybe by the first day of school everybody would forget about Mike's party.

Or I could quit school. Grandma could homeschool me. Then I wouldn't have to see any of those kids again except Mike.

By the time I got to my street it was almost dinnertime. My clothes were soaked with sweat. I just wanted go to my room. I didn't feel like talking to anybody. Then I noticed something was wrong.

When I first saw the ambulance I started running. My legs were already hurting but I didn't care.

I thought it was at first but the ambulance wasn't in front of my house. It was in front of Mr. Manlow's. It pulled away ringing the sirens just as I got there.

Grandma and Grandpa hugging each other on our front lawn. I forgot to mow it but Grandma wasn't noticing. My first thought was that Mr. Manlow died which was sad but I was so glad Grandpa was okay that I felt like singing a church song.

"Was Bob okay when you checked on him this morning?" Grandma asked as soon as she saw me. Then my gladness went away.

"Yeah," I said. "Why?" I was having a hard time catching my breath. Now my heart was beating even harder than it was before from walking and running because I was scared.

I didn't go in to see him that morning.

Mr. Manlow was dead and it was my fault.

Grandma couldn't tell I was lying. She stared across the yard. "He had a stroke, they think. I went over with some cookies and he was lying on the floor. The medic said he might have been there for hours."

"Is he okay?" My voice sounded squeaky. I thought I was going to have a stroke. Dirty Harry sat on the grass with a big *I told you so* look on his furry face. I couldn't believe I ever liked that dog.

Grandma shook her head. "I don't know, Matty. "

"Bob Manlow is a good guy," Grandpa said. Grandma led him and Dirty Harry back to our house. Grandpa looked over his shoulder and pointed his finger at me. "And you're a good boy," he said.

Grandpa wasn't right about me. Cassie was.

Gross.

4
How to Be Manly

The last thing I wanted to do the day after Mike's party and Mr. Manlow almost dying was get up at six in the morning to go to yard sales with my grandmother.

"Come on." She flicked my ear to wake me up. "I need you to drive."

"How can you think of yard sales at a time like this?" I grabbed a pillow and folded it over my head. "We should stick around and wait to hear from Mr. Manlow."

"I'll call the hospital when we get back. You have five minutes to be down in the car. I want to get the best deals before the selfish

52

people do."

"Doesn't that make you the selfish person?"

"There's a donut in it for you if you're down in less than five."

She left me to get dressed. My legs were so stiff from walking home from Mike's house that it hurt to put on my shorts. A big purple bruise spread out over the top of my knee and the places where my thighs touched were all red and peeled. All I wanted to do was sleep for five more hours. If I was asleep I couldn't think about Cassie or Mr. Manlow or flunking Algebra or anything about my stupid life.

Grandma called me from downstairs.

Normally, thinking about Cassie was all I ever wanted to do. If I was sitting in class or church or some other boring place I always thought about Cassie. I had this daydream that she would be walking along and a group of guys would start messing with her and scaring her. Then I would jump in and beat them all up. After I saved her she would kiss me for a long time because she would finally see that I was more than just a friend.

Now I didn't want to think of Cassie, but my brain just kept jumping back to her by habit. All I could hear was her voice calling me gross. Over and over again. I ran a brush over my head without looking at myself in the mirror. I did not want to see what she was talking about.

Grandma fanned herself with the list of addresses while I drove. She told me when to go left and right. We stopped at one house with a big front yard and about five tables loaded with stuff. The people were still taking books out of boxes and spreading them around. Grandma patted the fanny pack belted around her middle.

"This will be a good one. We're the first ones here."

"How can you be so happy about a yard sale when Mr. Manlow might be dead already?" I was in the worst mood of my life.

Grandma turned to look at me real slow from the passenger seat. "Want to try that again?"

"Sorry," I said. My face tingled even though I knew she would never hit me, even if I deserved it. "I'm just worried, okay?" I didn't say that I was worried that I might be a gross person inside *and* out. I didn't say what I was worried that if Mr. Manlow ended up dying, it would be all my fault. Maybe Mr. Manlow's ghost would haunt me at night. He might come through my window and say, *Why didn't you come check on me?* I would die of a heart attack on the spot if that happened.

Then I felt bad for thinking it. Mr. Manlow was a nice old guy. He wouldn't haunt me.

Grandma was quiet for a second like she was deciding whether or not to be mad. Then she sighed. "I'm worried too," she said.

"You are?"

"Of course I am. That man is living my

worst nightmare." She handed me a donut from the box between us. I took a bite and powdered sugar fell on the steering wheel. "After all, Bob's all alone. His wife died. He only had the one son, who passed away some years ago. It's lucky he moved in next door to us. He's lucky to have you checking in on him every morning and not just for his safety either. A man like that can get very lonely."

I sank lower in the seat. I only went in to say hello about half the times I said I did. It was easier to just say I went in than to actually have to go stand around in Mr. Manlow's kitchen while he asked if I wanted milk and rambled on about his son's football championship.

"Look," Grandma said. "Let's just see this one sale. After lunch you can come with me to the hospital for visiting hours."

"Yeah, okay."

"You're such a good boy, Matty. How many kids you know would care this much about an elderly neighbor?"

I got out of the car. I didn't want to hear anymore about what a good boy I was.

Grandma went straight for a table full of black Santa Claus statues. Grandma was a big believer in black Santa. I think if on Christmas Eve Grandma caught a white Santa coming down our chimney she'd send him right back up. She wasn't prejudiced or anything. She loved Grandpa and he was white. Grandma just thought that black Santa deserved a chance too. Whenever there was a black Santa statue at a yard sale it was always the first thing she grabbed.

The Christmas stuff didn't interest me. I shoved the rest of the donut in my mouth and stuck around the books. They had a million books about sports.

I brushed sugar off my hands and tried to find some science fiction. Then a title of one of the football books made me stop and pick it up. It was called *How to Be Manly*.

I looked around real fast to make sure that nobody saw me pick up a book called *How to Be Manly*.

There was a picture of the author on the front. He was a football player from when I was a little kid. He clutched a ball to his chest and he was about to run through a big mob of other players. I flipped through the pages. There were only a few pictures. The back said that he was an MVP for the Chargers.

I used to be a fat kid. A loser. I started reading the first couple lines and I couldn't stop. It was like I was hypnotized. *Girls wouldn't have anything to do with me. I had nothing to show for myself.* The guy's voice was right there in my head.

My father was a good man. He saw what was happening to me and he helped me become the person I am today. Through five simple steps, my father showed me how to be strong, successful and rich. He showed me how to be a man. I owe everything to him. If you aren't getting what you want out of life, let me share these five steps with you. Let me share with you How to Be Manly.

"You can have a whole bag full of books for a dollar."

I jumped. A lady with a visor leaned across the table and held out a plastic bag. "I'm not reading this," I said.

"It looks like you are," she said.

"Well I'm not." I dropped the book like it was hot.

"That author grew up around here," the lady said. "He went to the high school. Played ball in his senior year as I recall."

"I never heard of him," I said. That didn't mean anything. I never watched sports.

"I think he died in a wreck or something like that," the lady said. "Such a sad story." She picked *How to Be Manly* up off the pile and handed it back to me. "Are you sure you don't want it?"

I scooted over to my grandmother.

"Find anything you want to read?" she asked. The black Santa statues clanked together in her arms. They looked up at me like they were her babies.

"No way," I said. I took the Santas and carried them to the car while she paid the lady in the visor. On my way past the book table, I swiped *How to Be Manly* and stuck it under my shirt.

***

Mr. Manlow looked like a dead man. His cheeks sunk in and his mouth hung open while he slept. Wires and tubes stuck out all over the place. Grandpa and I sat by his bed without talking. The gadgets around the bed beeped and whispered.

Grandma was down the hall visiting a lady from our church that just had surgery. Grandma was always visiting people in the hospital or bringing them food after they got out. It was her favorite thing. I wished she would come back.

Mr. Manlow woke up. He blinked his eyes. "Well, well," he said. "Hello, friends."

"Hello, friend," Grandpa said.

Grandma came in then. She kissed Mr. Manlow on the forehead. "We thought you had a stroke," she said.

"No stroke," he said. "Just a fall. Fractured my hip. Then fainted like a pansy." He chuckled.

I looked out the window. The hospital was right by the freeway. I pretended to look at the cars. Maybe if I kept quiet they would forget about me and how I said I checked in with Mr. Manlow when I didn't.

"Hello, Matthew," Mr. Manlow said. Grandma hit me with her elbow. I sat up.

"Hey," I said.

"How's Dirty Harry?"

"He's good." I had actually walked him without the car when we got back from the yard sale.

"They're shipping me off to convalescent care in a couple days. I won't be home for at least six weeks," he said. "I'll need you to look after my dog for me while I'm gone."

I nodded.

"Do you remember when you fell, Bob?" Grandma asked. "It must have been after seven-thirty. Matty said you looked fine in the morning."

My face was about to burst into flames. Grandma was going to know I lied. She was going to know that I left Mr. Manlow alone in his house even while his own dog was trying to tell me that something was wrong.

I closed my eyes and waited.

Mr. Manlow cleared his throat. I thought I was going to puke.

"It must have been some time after that," he said. "I don't remember exactly."

I opened my eyes. I should have been relieved but there was something about the way Mr. Manlow looked at me that made me wish the truth had come out instead. He looked at me with his clear green eyes like he knew everything about me. And I mean everything.

"I'll look after Dirty Harry, don't worry about that," I said. "And I'll check on your house if you want."

"That's fine," Mr. Manlow said. He sounded tired again even though he just woke up. He told me where to find his house key. When it was time to leave he held out his hand for me to shake. His grip was stronger than I expected.

"Don't give me a limp fish, boy," he said. He wouldn't let me go. "You can tell a lot about a man from his handshake."

I was afraid of breaking his fingers. I squeezed back and pumped my arm a couple of times.

"Better," he said. He smiled at me. We shared a secret. I was a liar and he was the only one who knew it. I made my grip stronger. I couldn't say what I was thinking with Grandma there, but I hoped Mr. Manlow got it. I was sending messages through the handshake: *I'm making it up to you. I'm making up for what I did and what I didn't do.*

***

Jester was waiting on our front porch when we got home. His skateboard was propped on the steps and he was stretched out across Grandpa's couch.

"Hey Fatty," he said. Grandma clicked her tongue against her teeth.

"What are you doing here?" I asked.

He shrugged. "I don't know. Just came to say hey." He acted like he had forgotten what happened at Mike's pool party. He jumped and grabbed the rain gutter poking out from the porch overhang. "Dude. Your house is falling apart. So you want to go do something or what?"

"I can't right now," I said, clenching my teeth.

"Seriously. The roof is trashed." He pulled on the metal gutter so that it bent even more.

I pushed his hand away. "Knock it off, Jester!" I said.

"Boys," Grandma's voice was full of warnings. She gave Jester the evil eye like she wanted to yell at him but she couldn't because it was time to take Grandpa inside. Grandpa needed his dinner. If he didn't stay on his schedule he could get in a bad mood.

"What the hell?" Jester rubbed his hand where I hit it.

"How about what you did to me at Mike's yesterday?" I said once Grandma was inside. "You made me look like a pervert in front of Cassie."

"Bro, that was hilarious." He blinked at me like he truly did not understand why I was mad.

"No, it wasn't," I said. "It actually really sucked."

"Maybe if you didn't run off like a big baby," he said. He tipped up his skateboard with his toe and picked it up. "Come on, man. Don't be a girl. Let's go to 7-Eleven. I'm buying."

Jester always had money for whatever we wanted. Part of me wanted to go with him. We could just forget about what happened at Mike's. We would walk downtown so that Jester could make fun of everybody we saw on the way. We would get Slurpees and chips and then go to the park where I'd watch him do tricks at the skateboard ramps. He would pay for anything and never ask me to pay him back. It would be as though nothing changed.

But then I thought about how stupid I felt sprawled out on top of Cassie. It was the most embarrassing thing that ever happened to me in my entire life. I would be lucky if she ever called me or said hello in the halls again.

Forget about her ever seeing me as more than a friend. My stomach twisted up in a knot. It wasn't fair. Jester was my friend. Raining cash on me would never solve the problem. He was supposed to have my back.

"Forget it," I said. "Maybe some other time. I don't know."

I tried to push the gutter back into place. It just fell down worse. Grandpa used to take care of the house. Grandma said we couldn't afford to get somebody to fix the rain gutters and the roof yet. We had to save the money so that we could pay someone to do it for us. The roof problems were not things I knew how to begin to fix.

I had enough problems. I didn't need Jester giving me crap about my house. I went inside after Grandma so that he was left standing on the porch by himself. He swore like he didn't care if Grandma heard him, slapped his skateboard on our driveway and rolled away. I wondered who he was planning on hanging out with since I rejected him. Sometimes I saw him in the park with guys that were older than us. I don't even think they went to school anymore. They were the kind of guys where you didn't have to ask any questions to know to stay as far away as possible.

"I don't like Jesse calling you names," Grandma said when I came into the kitchen. She mixed homemade macaroni and cheese in a big pot.

"He's just trying to be funny. Like always." I sat down next to Grandpa. He squinted over the newspaper. I wondered how much he still got out of it. I handed him his reading glasses and he thanked me. He was off his eye patch, which made me glad. He liked it but it made him look too different.

"He's not as funny as he think he is," Grandma said. "If calling names is how he gets his laughs."

Grandpa grabbed my right hand.

"You are not Fatty," he said.

"I know, Grandpa," I said. I patted his knuckles. Then I noticed that his eyes were clear as though a breeze had just blown through the clouds that had covered them. It wasn't just the cataracts that were gone. He was there with me.

"You are not Fatty," he said again. His voice was strong and sure like it used to be when I was a little kid. Grandma looked up from stirring.

"Your name is Matthew," he said. He put his other hand on the back of my neck. It was like he was back after being gone from us for such a long time. He pulled me towards his face so that our foreheads were touching. "You are our Matthew. And you are a very, very strong young man."

Grandma saw what was going on right away. She came over and put her arms around both of us. Sometimes Grandpa came back to us all of a sudden like that. The doctors warned us that it would never last long.

Grandma and I stayed very still like Grandpa was a delicate butterfly that had just landed in the kitchen. We didn't want to scare him away.

"I love you," Grandma whispered, her face pressed into his cheek. "Oh my love."

After a few minutes Grandpa's eyes glazed over and he nodded off sitting at the table. I brought him to his easy chair in front of the television and Grandma went back to stirring. She was sniffing and I asked if she was okay.

"Something in my eye is all," she said.

I knew it was more than that but Grandma never cried. She liked to be strong. I would be strong too. Somehow I would find a way to be the kind of person Grandpa thought I already was. Maybe the book I got at the yard sale would help me do that. Grandpa's eyes were open but faded again. They reflected the television screen.

So my father and grandfather weren't exactly in a position to help me out. Who was to say a book couldn't help me? I went upstairs to start reading *How to Be Manly*. At least it was worth a try.

It ended up being a really good book.

It ended up changing everything.

5
Manly Body

The next morning after church, I went straight to my room to read.

You must begin with a manly body. To have a manly body, you must have low body fat, strength, agility and speed. Our ancestors didn't sit around watching television all day, and neither should you. Today is the first day of the rest of your life. Put down the donut and let's get going.

A big fat donut bar sat on a napkin on my bed. Tad Manly was talking straight to me. Grandma always got me a donut on the way back from church. It was tradition. She let me get the frosted bars on Sunday even though they were more expensive. They spread the glossy chocolate glaze extra thick this morning. It was winking at me.

Put down the donut...

My pants wouldn't button up when I got dressed before church. I had to lie down flat to zip them. When we got to church we sat across the pew from Coach Grimes and Jessica and Jessica's mom. Jessica waved at me but all I did was nod. I was afraid that if I lifted up my hand to wave back my jacket would rip. I hated to tell Grandma but I was going to need bigger church clothes too. Suit pants were way pricier than jeans.

I couldn't wait until it was time to go home and change into my shorts and get back to reading. In the black and white photos of Tad from when he was in high school he was even fatter than me. His pudgy neck overflowed his collar. In one school picture he smiled at the camera like a happy guy but according to the book he hated life when he was a kid. People used to tease him at school and they bullied him to the point that he wanted to drop out in the ninth grade.

You need to stop sitting around. Do something. Do something for yourself. Get so strong that nobody can push you around ever again.

I was glad at least I didn't get bullied. I wasn't the only big kid at school. A lot of people were heavy. It wasn't just me.

But then I thought about what happened at Mike's party with Jester and Cassie and I wondered if it was true that I never got bullied. Jester was supposed to be my friend. I got called Fatty Matty all the time and it hardly ever bothered me. But Jester pushed me over like I was as just another one of his stupid jokes. If someone like me liked a girl, it was a big joke for everybody to laugh at.

How much I loved Cassie did not feel like a joke to me.

I closed my eyes and brought her up in my mind. In the movie in my head her long hair blew in the breeze. She let me touch her shiny skin that smelled like coconut oil. Then I heard her call me *gross*.

I opened my eyes and faced the reality in the mirror on my bedroom wall. I knew I was XXL and not the most suave guy or whatever. But Cassie was supposed to be my friend too. She knew I wouldn't have landed on top of her on purpose. She didn't have to call me that.

I hated thinking about her now. Tad Manly was right. I needed to stop sitting around and do something.

I wrapped the donut in a napkin and tossed it into the wastebasket near my desk. It smelled up my whole room. I wanted to eat it more than anything. It would take forever for me to lose weight. It wouldn't matter if I just ate that last donut.

I fished it out of the garbage and brushed off a few pencil shavings that stuck to the frosting. I took a bite but after about four chews I spit the wet dough back out in my hand.

When you start this program, your whole life will change. Suddenly you will be capable of things you never thought possible. You will trade one way of doing things for another. You will look in the mirror and barely recognize the new, more manly you.

The garbage wasn't good enough. I brought the donut downstairs to put down the disposal in the sink. I needed it out of sight and out of mind, but I didn't want Grandma to know I didn't eat it. Wasted food made her mad. I ran cold water down the drain as the old disposal ground the donut out of my life. I had the same mixed up feeling as when I got rid of the milkshake. I was glad it was gone, but I felt bad too. I loved donuts. Donuts used to be my friends.

My grandparents sat in front of the television watching the preacher they liked.

Sunday was a day-long churchy holiday in our house.

I tightened the laces of my athletic shoes.

"Where you headed?" Grandma asked. Grandpa curled up on the couch beside her with his head resting on a pillow on her lap.

"Walking Dirty Harry."

"In this heat?"

"I'll maybe go in Mr. Manlow's pool after," I said. "If you don't think he'd mind."

"He said you could," she said. "You should go over there every day while Mr. Manlow's away. Make sure his flowers are watered and his house is clean while you're at it."

"Okay," I said. "I'll walk the dog first, though."

"Do you need me to hold the leash?" Grandpa said.

"No," I said. Tad Manly would think driving a dog around the block to get out of walking was the un-Manliest thing anybody ever heard of.

***

At first I started just walking Dirty Harry but he pulled on the leash. I guess he was nervous from Mr. Manlow being gone. He pulled so much that I thought I might as well run a little bit.

The problem was that running made me fart. I was okay for a couple of blocks but then my legs started to hurt and I kept passing gas. Every five steps or so I farted so loud that I couldn't believe people weren't coming out of their houses to check out the noise. It was a good thing that mostly old people who couldn't hear too well lived in my neighborhood.

I forced myself to not stop. The dog was happy and we got a rhythm going with my farts. He barked every now and then to show his support. We were like our own band.

I knew from driving Dirty Harry that one time around the block was just under a quarter mile. I made myself jog around five times. I did a mile run in school before. I was slow but I could do it. This time I wanted to push my limits. I kept telling myself that the next lap would be my last one but then I always did one more.

By the time I got back to Mr. Manlow's backyard the skin between my legs was on fire. It literally felt like I could start a campfire with the friction from my leg fat. I kicked off my shoes and pulled off my shirt and let myself fall into the pool. I sank to the bottom and sat there like a Buddha statue.

Underwater it was quiet. I decided right then that I was going to do everything Tad Manly said for the whole summer. I didn't care if it was the stupidest thing ever. Nobody had to know what I was doing or what I was reading. Guys like Jack or George at school who had all the girls liking them weren't better than me. There was no reason I couldn't have what they had. I pounded my fists against the bottom of the pool. My lungs hurt but I stayed under.

I was going to follow all the steps in *How to Be Manly*, but no one could know about it. Not even Grandma. I didn't have to explain what I was doing to anybody. And I sure as hell didn't want anybody making fun of me about it.

I kicked my way to the surface. My legs ached but I felt good, too. Running sucked but at least I wasn't thinking about Cassie when I was doing it. I kept swimming back and forth. As long as I was moving I felt okay.

***

At dinner I said no to Grandma's mashed potatoes. She didn't say anything about it until I said no to dessert. She held the cake knife up and looked at me as if I had lost my mind and said goddamn.

"What did you say, young man?"

"No cake for me, please."

Grandpa had no reaction. He nodded over his own slice of chocolate fudge with rainbow sprinkles like the cake had asked him a question.

I wished she wouldn't fight me on saying no to cake. I was still hungry after only eating chicken and salad but Tad Manly's directions on diet were pretty simple. *Say no to desserts. Most of your meal should be meat and vegetables with whole grains like brown rice. This is the kind of food that will give you the Manly body you're working for.* If Grandma was going to start fighting me about eating stuff I had a hard time saying no to in the first place, this was going to be a hard road.

"Is this because of what that long-haired nasty boy Jesse said to you yesterday? What was it he called you?"

"Fatty Matty," I said.

"That's right. Don't you let what that boy says change how you do things. I'm not having it." She slumped the cake slice onto a little plate and slid it in front of me.

"It's not because of the name," I said. "Kids call me Fatty Matty every day. It's my nickname."

"It's your nickname?" Grandma's eyebrows were doing the sharp little dance they do when she's getting mad.

"Seriously, Grandma. It doesn't bother me. It's just a name."

"How come you never told me they call you that at school? I'm going to talk to the principal."

"No," I said. I picked up my fork. "Look, I'm eating it, okay? Please don't call the principal. I'm telling you it never bothers me. I'm used to it."

The bite was too big and I choked. I had to take a drink of water. Grandma wasn't noticing. She was rinsing off the knife in the

82

sink and looking confused.

"Why do they say it for?" she asked. "Fatty Matty is not a nice thing to call someone."

"It's nothing," I said. "There are lots of kids at school who are fat as me. Some are fatter." I didn't tell her that my plan was to end the summer not fat at all. Maybe I would have six-pack abs like Tad Manly. Like Jack. I grabbed some of my stomach fat under the table. I needed to start doing sit ups every night.

"You're not that fat," Grandma said. "You're sturdy. My daddy was built like you. You're not going to lose weight because of what some fool decided to call you. I did not raise you that way. "

"Yes ma'am," I said.

"Are you trying to lose weight, Matty? Is that what it is?"

Grandpa looked up and nodded his head with a peaceful expression on his face as though he was agreeing with the both of us. He was having a quiet day. Grandpa wasn't the sturdy side of the family. He was always skinny, but in the past couple years he grew even skinnier. I stared at his hands. His wrists were so thin they looked breakable.

"Matty," Grandma said. "Answer me. Do you want to lose weight? Is that what you want?"

The cake smelled fudgy. The bite I swallowed didn't feel right in my stomach. What I wanted was to be somebody Cassie would like as a boyfriend. I wanted to be somebody who didn't look like a fool at pool parties, or flunk Algebra, or get caught in lies to Mr. Manlow. What I wanted was to not be gross.

I could not talk to Grandma about the things I wanted. These were my private thoughts and besides, if I did tell her she would get all mad at me and yell.

"Why can't we just drop it?" I asked.

"Because I did not raise you that way. I did not raise you to hate who you are." Her voice was telling me that pretty soon she was going to be mad anyway.

My shoulders hunched forward. I wished I could slide under the table and hide out there for a while like I did when I was a kid. Grandma started talking about loving myself but I wasn't feeling it. She didn't understand what I had to go through and if I told her she would go crazy. If I told Grandma that Cassie called me gross, then I wouldn't be allowed to talk to Cassie on the phone or even mention her name in the house ever again. Grandma would probably call Cassie's mom on the phone and give her a talk about manners. And I would die.

Grandma wasn't done. "The way I see it, you just don't respect yourself," she said. She stood in the middle of the kitchen with her hand on her hip. If I wasn't careful this was going to turn into an hour-long lecture.

"No it's not that," I tried to think fast. "It has nothing to do with what Jester called me. The reason why I said no to cake is that I'm thinking of going out for football. Like what Coach Grimes said in the mall."

"Oh," Grandma said. She smiled like someone turned on a light. "Why didn't you say so? I'll make the call tonight. I was hoping you would say so."

I smiled too but inside I started to panic. Coach Grimes was nice in front of Grandma but in school he was a boot camp general. The man yelled at people for nothing. If your shoes were untied in gym class he acted like he was one step away from calling the FBI. If your shirt wasn't tucked in, forget it. I might not survive the first day of practice.

Then again, I had gone for a run that afternoon in the sun and I didn't puke or die.

"Yeah," I said like I wasn't scared. "The football team."

"Really," Grandma said. She kept smiling.

She took away my cake and kissed me on the head.

"I thought you would say football is too dangerous," I said. Maybe she hadn't thought it all the way through and would change her mind about it and decide the issue for me. "With all the tackling people and getting hit on the head."

"I think it's nice you want to join something," she said. "You wear helmets, you know. And that Kyle Grimes is such a nice man."

Grandma got on the phone with Coach Grimes while she started the dishes. She tucked the phone between her ear and shoulder and laughed and talked like he was one of her church lady friends.

I was pretty much in shock. The whole day had been weird. I never thought that I would ever run by myself without a P.E. teacher forcing me. And I sure as hell never thought I would volunteer to join the football

87

team.

Maybe it wouldn't be so bad. Going out for football was a Manly thing to do, that was for sure.

I pushed Grandma out of the way with my elbow so I could finish the dishes for her. She patted my cheek with a soapy hand and went out into the living room.

"Matthew will be there at practice tomorrow morning," Grandma said. After she hung up the phone she squeezed my face in her hands. They smelled like Ivory soap. "You're a football player now, my big boy," she said.

I sat with Grandpa on the porch after I was done cleaning up. I didn't want Grandma to fuss over me anymore. I had to think for a minute. I was realizing what had just happened and it was crazy. Because what had just happened was that I chose to be on the football team in order to get out of eating dessert.

Grandpa waved at people walking by. Grandma came out and I got out of her regular place on the saggy old couch. They settled in for a long evening sit on the porch. Neighbors came up to say hello. Everything seemed normal but it wasn't. Nothing was like it used to be.

Suddenly you will be capable of things you never thought possible. Tad Manly said that in the first chapter of his book. So far it was true. I wasn't sure I liked it.

6
The Field

Blades of grass tickled my ear. So this is where I would die. The sun burned my eyes right out of their sockets.

"You okay, Matt?" Coach Grimes bent over me. His breath was minty. He was chewing gum. It was blue. How dumb that my last thought on earth before I died would be noticing that my Coach's gum was blue. On the last run at the sled I knocked my stomach into my lungs. Black spots danced around Coach's head. I wondered if he could see them too.

He held up a finger. I watched it go back

and forth. Then he pulled me up by my helmet face guard. My feet stayed under me.

"You're okay," he said. He smacked me on the butt. There was a lot of butt-smacking so far in football.

"I'm dying," I croaked.

"Nah," Coach said. "Just had the wind knocked out of you. Never had the wind knocked out of you before?"

"Uh."

Coach put his arm around me. "You're doing fine, Matt. Keep working. Keep working."

Then he pushed me back into line for drills.

This was where I lived now. Nothing else was real. I ran at the sled. There were purple jerseys and the sun in my eyes and green grass. A sea of green. Always green. The field never ended.

The sled. My enemy. It looked padded and cushy but that was a trick.

I ran at full speed. I never ran that fast in my life.

"Faster," Coach said. "Gut it out, Matthew. You're making your grandmother proud today." I slammed the sled with all my might and pushed at it until Coach blew the whistle.

I lurched off it, rubbing at the sore place on my stomach. My dad had never played sports. There were no trophies in the house. I could see why.

"You aren't getting more than you can handle out here," Grimes said. "Trust me."

I squinted against the sun. The man was not making any sense. I had more than I could handle from my first minute on the field. I had no idea what time it was or when I would be able to go home. I looked out at the street beyond the fence. I wondered what would happen if I made a break for it.

Coach crossed his arms in front of his chest with his eyes narrow as a snake's. If I wanted to run off the field I'd have to get past him first to do it. Grimes was a fat kid psychic. He always seemed to know what I was thinking.

The funny thing was that truthfully I didn't feel like leaving the field. Football sucked so far and I wasn't good at it but I felt kind of peaceful. On the field nothing mattered but the field. There were no worries. There were the yards to run and the sled to hit and the other guys to block.

My turn came up again to run up against the sled. I bent my head and charged.

***

Pain.

I lay in bed with a plastic bag of ice melting on top of my swollen ankle. Coach said to ice it. He said I'd be good for practice in the morning. This was a stone-faced lie because I was never going to walk again.

I didn't know why I ever thought the field was peaceful. I was okay until I got home and took a shower and rested. Then it was like my body snapped out of being in shock that I was exercising. Everything in and on my body hurt. My arms. My legs. After sleds we had to run across the field some more. Then up and down the bleacher stairs ten times. Or a million times.

I puked twice. It would have been embarrassing except that I wasn't the only one. I counted at least five other kids puking on the sidelines at different times in the practice.

"Grimes is the devil, man," George said while I bent over heaving the second time. Then he smacked me on the butt. He didn't call me Fatty Matty once.

Coach Grimes *was* the devil. He acted friendly but he only did that so he could kill you later. If I survived the night there was no way I could go back to the field the next day. Now I saw why my dad didn't do sports. We just weren't a sporty kind of family.

My ankle was so cold I could barely feel it. The swelling was going down. I wished it was broken. Then I would have an excuse Grandma and Coach would have to believe.

But Grandma had been so happy making me eggs and bacon that morning before practice. She sang along to the radio and kept rubbing my head and messing up my hair. Too bad all that breakfast ended up in the grass as fertilizer.

Tad Manly said in his book that every kid should be in sports. I was on flag football when I was a kid and I liked it but I was way faster back then. Not so big. It was easier to be a little kid. There were no four-hour practices with a loud and crazy devil on a field as hot as hell.

I thought maybe I should quit. Coach and Grandma would give me a hard time for a day or two but everybody would get over it.

Then my phone buzzed. It was a text from Cassie.

U on the team?

Yes. I was so tired my thumbs were shaky. Yeah, maybe I should quit.

Cool.

Then again... maybe I shouldn't.

7
Manly Mind

Mrs. Grant hit me on the head.

Only with a pencil, but still. Teachers aren't supposed to hit their students. I rubbed the top of my head and felt confused.

"No sleeping in my class, Matthew."

"Right," I said. I didn't know I had fallen asleep. I hadn't meant to.

"You can stand against the wall if you need," she said.

In order to walk Dirty Harry and water Mr. Manlow's lawn before football practice, I had to get up at five in the morning. I kept waiting for practice to get easier or for Coach to give us a break but he never did. Every day the workout was harder than the day before.

Today we had to do lunges back and forth across the field until some guys started rolling around on the grass with leg cramps. I felt sorry for those guys. One of the leg crampers was my friend Mike. Two days after I started football Mike joined the team too. When I asked him about it, he said if I could do it, he could do it. He didn't really want to talk about it. I guess it was Charity Month for Coach Grimes because Mike was even slower than me. And after a hundred lunges, Mike wasn't going anywhere. He clutched his leg while he rocked on the ground.

"You okay, man?" I tried to block the sun from his eyes with my head. Coach Grimes knelt to massage his calf.

"Uh," Mike said through grit teeth. Then he said the worst possible word in the cussing dictionary but Coach pretended not to notice. I guess leg cramps so bad they knock you down give you that kind of permission.

By the time I got home, I only had an hour to take a shower and eat lunch before I had to get back to school in time for Algebra. Grandma wasn't as mad at Mrs. Grant for flunking me as I thought she would be. In fact, she wasn't mad at her at all. After she opened up my report card she just left it on top of the bills and shook her head. If I thought she was going to stand up for me with Mrs. Grant, I was wrong. She said I had to go to summer school to take the class over again during the summer and stop complaining.

Grandma also said she wouldn't drive me there after practice because it was my own fault that I had summer school in the first place. Even though I did most of the driving in our family, Grandma's rule was that I couldn't go around by myself until I had a license. Besides, Grandma needed the car.

So that meant I had to walk Dirty Harry before sunrise, then ride my bike back and forth from school for football practice, and then back and forth again for Algebra class. I could have just stayed at school for the whole time and showered in the locker room, but then Grandma wouldn't get any break from looking after Grandpa. She needed that hour while I was home to deliver cakes or just to rest.

This wasn't the way summer was supposed to be.

Sleepiness dragged me down like quicksand. I went to the back of the class to stand. I crossed my arms and rested my head against the wall. I closed my eyes and thought about Cassie. Her long hair. Her laugh. The way she looked up at me from under her eyelashes and smiled. Now that we were on good terms again it was nice to be able to go back to my daydreams about Cassie.

I had this one daydream I was thinking about a lot lately. In this daydream I was walking through the halls of school on the first day of sophomore year and nobody recognized me. I was so buff from working out that nobody could call me Fatty Matty anymore. Cassie floated up to me in the hallway and put her arms around my neck and kissed me in front of everyone.

Then some guys would start bothering Cassie and I'd beat them up. When I was done, she would fly back into my arms and tell me she loved me. In front of everyone.

"Open your eyes, Matthew," Mrs. Grant said.

"Right," I said. My awesome daydream disappeared... Mrs. Grant's annoying voice blew it apart completely. I was in my same old math class. No Cassie in sight because she passed Algebra. Another two hours before I could go home.

"Keep them open," Mrs. Grant said. "You need to learn this."

Coach Grimes wasn't the only evil one. Mrs. Grant was the devil too.

***

I took a break and sat under a tree in the park to read a few pages on the way home. I didn't know if I'd have chores to do or if Grandma would need me to fix something. I might not have time to read until after dinner.

A Manly body is only the first step. You must also cultivate a Manly mind. This means doing your best in school. If you're out of school, you should still strive to learn. Be the most knowledgeable person you know. Read books the way you used to eat potato chips. Don't stop at just one.

When I got home from Algebra class I meant to jump into Mr. Manlow's pool for a while before starting in on my homework. I had a resolution to do all of my homework including the bonus questions. I was already getting everything back all A's. Mrs. Grant knew I didn't belong in summer school and I was proving it to her.

All of the heroes in the old stories don't just have physical strength. They have mental strength as well. When Hercules killed the Hydra, it wasn't enough to be so strong as to cut off all the heads. He had to be smart enough to think of burning the stumps to keep them from growing back.

I wished I'd found the Tad Manly book before school ended. Then I might have been inspired to do my homework and I wouldn't be stuck in four hours of summer school every day for six weeks.

I put my bike in the garage and pulled the door down. Grandpa slept on the porch couch while Grandma sat at the kitchen table doing the bills. Four perfectly iced cakes sat on the counter. She sold cakes to people she knew or who heard of her. She made cakes all the time. There was no escape from Grandma's cakes. They looked good but I forced myself to think of them as dog doo. If I told myself the frosting was dog doo then I wouldn't be tempted to lick the bowl Grandma left out for me. It would be a lot easier to believe it if the cakes didn't smell so awesome. When thinking of them as dog doo didn't work, it was easier if I just thought of not eating Grandma's baking as something I was going to do for that day. It wasn't like I had to give up cake forever. It was just a one-day thing.

This trick I played on myself was getting me through a lot of days.

I got a glass of milk and an apple before I noticed that something was wrong.

Grandma was crying. For real. Her head was down and her shoulders were shaking.

"Is everything okay?" I asked. It was a stupid question. Nothing was okay if Grandma was crying. Grandma never cried. It was coming out like a whisper. I ran back out to check if Grandpa was breathing. He swatted at me like I was a fly.

Back in the kitchen Grandma was up and wrapping up a casserole dish in aluminum foil.

Her eyes were red but that was it. I almost
didn't believe what I saw before.

"Is Mr. Manlow okay?" I asked.

"What?"

"Is he dead or something?"

"Matty! What a thing to say." She zipped
up her purse and put it over her shoulder. "I
visited Bob this morning. He's doing fine."

"Well then why were you crying?"

Grandma didn't answer. She smushed
the foil around the dish like she was afraid the
food would try to escape. "Be a good boy,
Matty. Look after Grandpa for an hour."

"Where are you going?"

"Mrs. Garvey's. She just got out of the
hospital. I'm just going to make sure she's set
up and then I'll come home." She wasn't
looking me in the eye.

"But you're crying," I said.

"I need you to put these cakes in boxes
for me, too. Be careful now. Stick them in the
fridge. We'll deliver them tonight if you don't

mind driving." She kissed me on the cheek and that was it. She left without saying another thing.

I sat in her chair at the table. The house was quiet except for Grandpa's snoring coming through the front window. If Grandpa and Mr. Manlow were fine, why was Grandma so upset? My mind went wild. Maybe she was the sick one. Maybe she'd just found out that she only had two months to live. My heart started beating hard. I couldn't take care of Grandpa by myself. And who would take care of me? I couldn't live without Grandma.

I picked up one of the papers on the table. It was a bank statement. I rubbed my eyes with my palm and looked it over. Then I looked it over again.

I saw why Grandma was crying.

***

My father's name is Daniel Sullivan. He

went to college for a couple of years after high school. Then he dropped out and came back to live at home with Grandma and Grandpa. He worked at fast food places for a while, then for restaurant in the mall. Grandma always called him a "late bloomer." Sometimes she said the same thing about me.

When Daniel was twenty he met a girl named Sherie. Sherie was my mom. I have a couple pictures of her. She was dark-skinned and she did not like to smile for the camera. That's about everything I ever knew about her. She moved in with my grandparents too for a while after she got pregnant with me. The way my grandparents always told it, the two meant to get married as soon as they were on their feet. My dad tried a bunch more jobs to see if he could find something he liked to do. He worked in a warehouse stacking boxes. He tried accounting classes.

Then my mother got sick and died. I was two years old and my father was already living in San Francisco, seeing if he could find better work to do there. He was going to get credits at a junior college then go to SF State. Sometimes when Grandma talked about him it made me think she still expected him to go to a university. I hated to tell her that I doubted that would ever happen.

I don't remember my mom. I used to close my eyes and try to remember as hard as I could but it never worked.

My grandparents were my real parents in almost every way. My dad came around more when I was a kid but my sixteenth birthday was coming up in a month and I hadn't seen him since he called me a mistake on my fourteenth. Grandma and I had a lot on our minds worrying about Grandpa and how to make him happy, and how to take care of the house by ourselves. I had school to think about and now football. I talked to Dad on the phone once in a while and I always asked if he could ever move in with us but he always said no. He had a job he couldn't leave.

It would be easier for us to have him around. He didn't have to live in San Francisco. We had jobs in our town too. Grandma and I could use help around the house and with Grandpa. Dad either didn't understand that or he didn't care. Sometimes it was like I didn't even have a father.

Except that I did. And he had just taken money out of their joint account. Not a little bit of money, either. A great big chunk of money. He left us with nothing in the balance. Less than nothing. There was a big minus sign. Grandma was going to have to pay a fine, it said.

I went down the numbers again. Then I looked through the bills open on the table. I picked up a pencil and made a list of numbers. Everything we owed. Everything Grandma and Grandpa took in with Social Security and their pensions. Before they retired, Grandma was a teacher and Grandpa was an engineer and worked for the state. She'd explained to me before that they had to be careful with money but they would always have enough to get by. We would always be okay.

She always told me not to worry.

I added up the numbers. I worried.

***

Grandma was later coming home than she'd said. I put away the cakes and finished the dishes that were in the sink and vacuumed the living room. I made everything nice and straight the way she liked it. The black Santas from the yard sale were still sitting on the counter in a row. I wondered if Grandma knew when she bought them that my dad was going to take out all of her money. She might have saved her quarters. I didn't even know that they had a joint account. Grandma never talked about it.

The Santas looked up at me with their

big brown eyes. If only one of them would come to life and throw a bunch of cash down our chimney. A little Christmas in June would be great.

Somebody knocked at the door. It was Jessica Grimes. She peeked through the screen holding a big binder to her chest.

"Hey," she said. "My dad wanted me to bring over the playbook for you to study this week."

"Just a second," I said. I'd almost forgotten that it was time to get Grandpa to come inside. He needed his afternoon snack and pills and water. He was snoozing on the couch on the porch. Grandma's bank statements made me forget to take Grandpa to the bathroom.

I helped him down the hall. It should have been embarrassing to do this with a girl in the other room but it wasn't for some reason. Jessica waited in the kitchen. She got a glass of water.

"Your faucet is leaking," she called.

"I know," I said. Whenever you turned on the cold, water seeped out from the handle. It had been that way for a long time. Grandma didn't know anything about plumbing and neither did I.

"Come on, Grandpa," I said. "Anything coming out?"

Grandpa didn't have to go. That wasn't a good sign. I left him out too long without something to drink. I led him back to the kitchen and he stood by while I fixed him an ice water and cookies. He ate the cookies standing up.

"I want to go for a walk," he said, spitting out crumbs. I handed him the glass and reminded him to take a long drink.

"Later, Grandpa," I said. "When the sun goes down and it's cooler we'll walk together. How's that."

"I want to go for a walk," he said again. He ate slow. When he was done I put on the golfing channel and let him sit in front of the T.V. for a while. Grandma didn't like him to watch too much T.V. during the day but I thought it would be okay in an emergency.

Jessica had set the playbook down on the table on top of the mess of bills and papers.

"So my dad wants you to memorize the first five plays by next Monday," Jessica said. She looked around at the paper avalanche.

"Right," I said. I opened up to the first page of the playbook. It was a list of directions and a diagram. I let out a long breath.

"Anything wrong, Matt?"

"Naw. It's just," I ran my hands over my head and realized that I was about to cry too. I might not have known much about money but I knew what a negative balance looked like. I knew what a minus sign meant. I squeezed my eyes shut.

"Is everything okay with your grandfather?" she asked. "My dad told me that he was sick. That must be hard."

"Grandpa is okay. He's been better lately. That's not it."

"Well something is wrong, I can tell," she said. Her fingertips brushed my hand.

"So I guess Coach isn't the only one who can read my mind," I said.

"What?"

I shook my head again. I didn't know what I was saying. I was trying to be funny but it wasn't coming out right. I couldn't fall apart. My crying like a baby wasn't anything anybody needed. But without thinking I grabbed one of Grandma's Santas and got ready to throw it against the wall.

Jessica caught me before I could do it. She yanked the Santa out of my hand. She didn't let go of my arm either.

"You better tell me what's going on right about now," she said.

So I did. We sat down and I showed Jessica everything in the bank statements. It would have been great if she found some reason why it wasn't as bad as it looked. Maybe there was a reason why a man would take that amount of cash out of an account and leave his parents and own kid poorer than dirt.

She took eyeglasses out of her back pocket and slipped them on to read. She looked serious and older than me even though we were the same age.

"This is bad," she said, scooting Grandma's Santa out of my reach. "But leave poor Santa Claus out of it. It's not his fault."

"I don't know what to do," I said.

"You're not alone, Matt. Whatever is going on, you've got friends around to help."

I didn't want to hurt her feelings but the truth was I didn't have many friends. I had Mike and Jester and lately I wasn't sure of them.

Jessica didn't say anything else for a while and she was cool with me not talking either. She looked at the wall like she was thinking. We sat quietly and listened to the people clapping on Grandpa's golf game on the television.

***

By the time Grandma came back, Jessica had already left. Her mom expected her home for dinner. I didn't know Jessica very well, but I was glad she came over with the playbook when she did. She had given me a list of things to say to my grandmother, which I needed because I didn't know how to bring any of it up without Grandma shooting me right back down.

Grandma asked where Grandpa was and I said in the living room sleeping. She looked tired while she fussed around the kitchen. She filled a pot with water from the leaky faucet and put it on the stove to boil. Grandpa's game show was ringing. Somebody had won something.

"What are we having?" I asked.

"Spaghetti." She went about stacking the bills and putting them in a cardboard box she kept for that stuff.

Everything in the kitchen seemed different. I always took it for granted that she had everything under control. There was nobody as strong as Grandma, not that I knew. Now I noticed that the wallpaper was peeling off by the stove. The floor sagged by the refrigerator, which itself needed to be pushed extra hard to close. This wasn't the way it was supposed to be. An old lady shouldn't have been the only one taking care of everything.

When Grandma came back from putting the bills away, I looked down at the piece of binder paper with the conversation starters Jessica wrote out for me.

"Grandma, I noticed when I came in earlier that you seemed upset. Would you like to talk about what was happening there?"

Grandma cut her eyes at me while taking a jar of sauce down from the shelf. "No, I would not. It's nothing for you to worry about."

Back to Jessica's list. I cleared my throat. "Sometimes a person's problems can feel overwhelming. Please tell me what I can do to help."

"Why are you talking like a robot, Matty?" She grabbed Jessica's paper out of my hands before I could hide it. She read it over, her lips moving in whispering lines.

"What is this?" she said.

"I know Dad's been stealing your money," I said. "I saw the statements."

"It's not your business, Matty."

"You're the one who left out all the stuff from the bank. How am I not supposed to look?"

"I told you not to worry." She went back to the sink.

"Stop telling me not to worry. I'm not a

baby. I can see what's going on," I said.

Grandma spun around. She looked mad. I didn't know what was going to happen. Grandma's mouth got tight like she was about to yell at me good.

Then she looked over my head into the living room. "Where's your grandfather?" she asked, pushing past me. I followed her. I expected Grandpa to be in his chair in front of the television. The last time I'd checked on him was right after Jessica left. But he wasn't there. His chair was empty and so was the couch. I ran to the porch but he wasn't at his place.

We looked in the bathroom. We looked in every room of the house. The game show rang again, crazy bells to show that it was somebody's lucky day.

There was no more mad at all in Grandma's face. Just a wide-eyed look that was way worse than the crying.

8

Lost Man

Grandma called the church. I ran around the neighborhood calling for Grandpa. Pretty soon a bunch of the neighbors were looking for Grandpa, calling his name. Then Reverend Foster joined us. A bunch of other people from church came over, including Jessica and her parents. Coach Grimes dropped Jessica and her mom off at my house and then went to search for Grandpa from his truck.

I tried to figure out how long he must have been gone before Grandma noticed he was missing. When I last checked on him he was sleeping in front of the TV right after Jessica left in the afternoon. When Grandma came back it was almost an hour later.

I called for him again. My voice caught in my throat. I started to run. He'd wanted to go for a walk but I'd made him wait. It was too hot when he wanted to go. He was an old man and he got thirsty and forgot to take drinks. I should have sat with him. I shouldn't have stuck him in front of the television.

He wouldn't be able to handle wandering around alone for long. He would get scared and lost in no time.

He had to be around the next corner. I knew that if I turned the next corner he would be shuffling down the sidewalk. I pumped my legs and forced myself to run faster. But at the corner he wasn't there. Nobody was there. The long strip of concrete sidewalk shone blinding white in the evening sun like a road to no place.

I called Grandpa's name. I called his name over and over.

***

The police called Grandma after eight at night. The sun was already down. Grandma got me on my cell phone. A jogger found Grandpa on the canal trail. He'd fallen and hurt his face so she called an ambulance to bring him to the hospital.

By the time I got home, Reverend Foster had already started the phone tree to call off the search. I thought of Coach Grimes driving around in his big old truck. It turned out that Grandpa wasn't even by the roads. He was a mile down the canal trail lying on the ground when the lady found him.

Reverend Foster, Grandma and I went out to the car to go to the hospital. I took the keys from Grandma and went to the driver's side out of habit.

"Son?" Reverend Foster said. "What are you doing there? Do you have your license?"

I stood with my fingers under the door handle. Grandma and I looked at each other like we were a couple of guilty kids. I was too tired to explain. I handed the keys to Reverend Foster and got into the backseat like I was somebody's son.

***

Grandpa's face looked worse than it was, the doctor said. An ugly scrape oozed blood from his forehead down to his chin. His hands and forearms were thrashed too. There was blood on his hospital gown. They had given him sleeping pills so he couldn't wake up to see us. I held his hand. I wanted him to wake up just for a second. I knew he was alive. His hand was warm and his chest rose and fell with his breathing. I just wanted to say hello for one second.

But he wouldn't wake up. The pills were too strong.

"He needs rest," the nurse said. "He's very weak. Let him be." She tried to pull my hand away but I pushed her away. Grandpa used to throw me over his shoulder and call me a sack of potatoes. He used to take Grandma and me on trips to the river and let me ride on his back while he swam from bank to bank. The nurse did not know what she was talking about. Grandpa was not weak. He was the strongest man in the world.

The doctor told Grandma about what we would need to do when Grandpa went home. They wanted to keep him in the hospital for a couple of days. Grandpa was dehydrated and exhausted, the doctor said. We needed to use this time to think about what we were going to do to take better care of him. Maybe we needed to start thinking of putting him in a home where he could have full-time nurses attending him. He'd be safer there.

I patted Grandpa's hand when what I felt like doing was punching a hole in the wall and yelling at the doctor to shut the hell up. We took great care of Grandpa. He was happy most of the time because of us. He didn't belong anywhere but at home with Grandma and me.

"He's getting to be too much for you," the doctor said.

"I'll find a way to take care of things," I whispered in Grandpa's ear. "Don't worry about anything. I'm smart and I'm going to figure this out."

If Grandpa was awake he would believe that I could.

9
Manly Spirit

I was up late with Grandpa at the hospital. I only got four hours of sleep before I had to get up for walking the dog, football practice and summer school. I fell asleep again sitting up in Algebra class. Mrs. Grant woke me when she slapped a graded test on my desk. There were barely any red marks on the paper, except for the big fat A scrawled across the top.

"You're acing this course, you know," she said. "I'm recommending you for Honors Geometry in the fall."

Mrs. Grant gave good news in the

same bright cheerful way she gave bad news. I
wondered if I was still asleep and dreaming but
it seemed rude to ask.

***

I circled the parking lot of the school a
couple of times on my bike after class got out.
Even though I was tired, I wasn't in the biggest
hurry to get home. The house was going to be
weird without Grandpa there. I had to figure
out what to say to Grandma about the money
problem. I had to ask in the right way or she
wouldn't tell me anything. Not that I knew what
to do if she told me everything. The whole
situation was bad.

No kids played in the park. The metal
slides on the play structures reflected the sun,
too bright to look at. Even the skaters stayed
away in the middle of the day. I rested in an
island of shade from a skinny tree by the
ramps. No one was around, so I took the book

out of my backpack. It was risky to even have it on me. Anyone who saw me reading *How to Be Manly* would think I was a freak. But I was glad I brought it. It sounds strange to say a book made me feel better about how screwed up my life was, but this one did.

Do not neglect your spiritual side. Whether you believe in God or not, you have a spiritual side. Make time in the week to go to church, or walk in nature. At least make time to pray every day. If you don't want to pray, meditate. A large part of my success on the field had to do with growing my spiritual side as well as my physical and mental strength. It's all connected.

I was on the chapter about Manly Spirit. Tad Manly thought that a man was made up of three parts: body, mind and spirit. According to Tad Manly, all three parts were equally important. You needed to be strong in all areas or it wasn't any good. I never thought about my spirit being a man's spirit. I just went to church when I was supposed to and forgot about it.

My father always told me to remember where I came from, and where I came from was God. Because of my father, I always remember to say a prayer of thank you every time something goes right, and also when something goes wrong. There's a lesson to be learned in everything. Take a walk in nature once in a while. Don't forget to say thanks for everything. Whether you believe in God or not, remember to say a big Thank You every single day.

I had the church part down, whether I wanted to or not. Grandma made us go no matter what. I didn't mind it, but it wouldn't matter if I did. I was going.

There was lots of music at my church and Reverend Foster was pretty entertaining most of the time. I prayed now and then but it never did any good. I prayed for Grandpa to get better and for Cassie to like me and I was still waiting on all of that. Maybe God was mad at me for always being obsessed over Cassie. Maybe I was being punished for having a dirty mind.

The kind of praying Tad Manly was talking about was different anyway. He was talking about saying thank you instead of asking for things.

Maybe I needed to take a walk in nature to get what Tad Manly was talking about. But I already exercised for four hours that day. I'd already been through a Grimes practice and two bike rides to and from school. I didn't feel like going for a walk. Besides, there wasn't any nature around where I lived. It was mostly mini malls and houses and big buildings downtown. I was sitting under the one bony little tree in the whole skate park and it wasn't giving me any answers.

I lay back and looked up through the leafy branches and tried to think of something to say a big Thank You for. I couldn't think of anything.

***

Grandma was at the kitchen table with the bills again when I got home. Grandpa's couch on the porch was empty. The cushions were dented from where he always lay. It was time for his afternoon nap. He should have been on the porch sleeping in the cool shade like normal. I hated that he wasn't home with us. If it weren't for me he would have been home where he belonged.

I was in a bad mood and I should have known better. I should have gone straight to my room but I didn't. I sat down across the table and tried to make Grandma talk to me.

"You need to tell me what's going on," I said.

"Check that tone, young man. I don't need to tell you anything." She didn't look up from her calculator but she started pushing the buttons harder.

"What are we going to do if my dad keeps stealing your money, Grandma?"

"He's not stealing it. He knows he can take what he needs."

"What's he need that much for? He works, doesn't he? He has a job. He doesn't even come visit." I sat up straight. I had to be ready for the truth.

"Not your concern," she said.

My hands were shaking. Grimes had us doing push ups until we literally couldn't do another one. If somebody offered any one of us a million dollars to do just one more, no one would be able to do it. I wanted to get a diet Coke from the fridge but I didn't think I'd have the strength to lift the can. Now that we were talking about it I didn't care if Grandma got mad at me. I wanted her to get mad. It would be better than pretending everything was okay when it wasn't.

"Grandma, what's going on?"

"Not your concern," she said again.

"If we end up homeless then what will you say?"

She reached out lightning fast and smacked me on the face. Then she held up one finger right by my nose. Her eyes were wet.

"Not your concern," she said. Again.

I blinked. Grandma hadn't raised her hand to me since I was little and she had to spank me for running into the street. She never hit me in the face. My heart pounded in my ears. I did not know what was happening to us.

Then a bomb exploded from somewhere above our heads.

At least, that's what I thought it was. Grandma ducked. I grabbed her and covered her with my body.

The window was bending in half and coming into the house. I pulled Grandma close to me so that I stood between her and whatever was happening. I pushed her out of the kitchen.

There was a whine and a crack and the front window crashed into the kitchen in a spray of glass. A cloud of dust blasted through.

It was over in a few seconds and then there was quiet. I held my arm out so that Grandma would stay safe behind me.

The porch overhang had fallen in a huge block of plaster, wood and roofing tiles. It blocked the window. White dust and glass covered the kitchen floor. Glass tinkled as shards fell from the broken panes. Dirty Harry was barking like crazy in our back yard.

I didn't try to go out the front door. I ran out the back and around the house from the side gate. The overhang pancaked on top of the porch. The place where Grandpa would have been having his afternoon nap was crushed under a broken slab of plaster and a pile of shingles. The edges of Grandpa's couch poked out from under the debris.

Grandma followed me out, grasping for the back of my shirt. I held on to her and she clung to me like she would fall down if I let go. "Praise God," she said. She buried her face in my shoulder and slapped my chest and just kept saying that one thing over and over like a prayer of thanks.

10

The Work of Men

Reverend Foster looked over the damage and rubbed his chin. He wiped his forehead with a hanky. Then he went back to rubbing his chin.

"Well Sister Vanessa," he finally said to Grandma. "You've got a problem here."

Grandma's mouth was a straight line. The three of us stood on the sidewalk looking at the big mess as if it was somebody else's house. If I could pretend it was not our house, then I could pretend that it didn't matter. The porch was demolished. I knew Grandma was looking at the bits of couch sticking out, thinking about what would have happened if Grandpa had been home taking his nap. I knew that was what she was thinking because it was what I was thinking.

"I think it's time you realized you are in over your head with this house," Reverend Foster said. "You need to let your church family help you."

"Oh," was all my grandmother could say. Then her mouth went back into the line.

We spent the night at Reverend and Mrs. Foster's house. Grandma got the guest room and I slept on the couch. The clock on the mantel ticked so loud I couldn't fall asleep. I spent most of the night staring at the different shapes the leaves from the trees outside the window made on the ceiling.

It was up to me to do something to stop all of the bad things from happening, but I didn't know what I was supposed to do.

I missed Grandpa. Not the Grandpa who acted like a kid and who lay confused and drugged on a hospital bed. I missed the Grandpa who took care of Grandma and me when I was younger. I missed the Grandpa who spent weekends around the house with a tool belt on. Fixing things. He made us feel so safe we didn't even realize everything he did until his mind started to fade away. I never thought about asking him to teach me how to do any of the fixing around the house. When I was a kid I took it for granted that he would always be there. Now it was too late and it wasn't fair.

Maybe Grandpa was nervous in the hospital without Grandma and me. When I was a kid Grandpa came into my bedroom whenever I had bad dreams. I always knew to call for him over Grandma because he never got cranky about me waking him up. He would sit on the edge of my bed for as long as I needed him. His bathrobe was soft and smelled like toothpaste and aftershave. When Grandpa was there I could not be afraid of anything.

The shadows on the ceiling moved and

danced like living things. Now that his brain was going, a shadow of Grandpa was all I had left. If he was home when the roof fell, I would have lost even that.

***

The next day it seemed like half the church was at our house. Reverend Foster rented a truck to load hunks of porch and roof to the dump. He handed me a pair of work gloves. I was glad to have something to do. I ran back and forth carrying wood and shingles from the porch to the back of the truck for hours. When we uncovered the smashed-up couch a group of ladies brought Grandma inside the house. She didn't need to see that. They distracted her with talk. Their old lady chatter and laughing bubbled through the broken windows like it was a party we were throwing.

In the middle of the afternoon, Coach

and Jessica came over with big trays of barbeque and potato salad for everybody from one of my favorite restaurants downtown. Jessica and I sat with our plates of food on the cool grass in the front yard. She handed me a water bottle and I drank the whole thing without stopping to take a breath.

Mr. Parker was one of the church members and he was a building contractor. Mr. Parker stood in front our house with the Reverend and Coach Grimes and some of the other men to talk about what still needed to be done. With the mess cleared out, it didn't look so much like a bomb had hit our house. The windows were broken and the front looked kind of bald and strange without the overhang. Based on the huge noise when it came crashing down I thought the damage would be worse. It seemed impossible after that explosion that we still had a house standing to live in.

"You have sauce on your face," Jessica

said. She wiped my chin with a napkin.

"Thanks," I said.

We pulled at blades of grass while we ate ribs. Jessica picked a pile of white clovers and buried my toes in them. They tickled but I left them there. I didn't feel like talking but I was glad Jessica had come by. It was nice to not be surrounded by a bunch of grown people barking orders for just a minute.

Before they left, Coach told me I could take a couple days off practice if I needed to stick around home and help rebuild the roof. He had a funny look on his face. I didn't know what to say. He made me nervous when he was being nice.

Jessica waved from the car as they drove away. I wasn't glad she was leaving. I waved back. I had a funny feeling in my stomach that wasn't from the barbeque. I didn't have time to think about it. Mr. Parker slapped me on the back and said there was work to be done. He handed me a hammer and a tool belt with pockets full of nails.

"Got more hours of building ahead of us," he said. "You've been a big help so far, Matthew. Not a single complaint all morning. We've been very impressed with you."

I didn't know what to say. It was weird to get a compliment like that. If he knew more about me he wouldn't say it. Reverend Foster came up beside him.

"We're patching this up in two days, praise God," Reverend Foster said. "Brother Parker says that with seven of us working hard, we can get it done."

I let them lead me back to the group of men.

***

The next day my back hurt and my shoulders ached. My ears rang with the sound of pounding hammers. Even after we finished, the hammers still banged in my head.

As soon as we were done the men from the church packed up their toolboxes and went home. They still had a few hours left of their Saturday. It was good to get done before sundown.

Grandma sat on the brand new couch. The ladies had taken her shopping for it that morning while we were rebuilding the porch and the roof. It was made of wicker and the cushions creaked when we sat down on them. I missed the old couch but I didn't say anything.

I sat on the newly built front steps. The fresh lumber of the planks smelled good to me. Grandma had put a glass of cold lemonade in my hand but I was too tired to drink it.

Only Mr. Parker stayed behind. He held a clipboard with a list of repairs our house still needed.

"How much do I owe you for labor and materials?" Grandma asked.

"This one's on me, Mrs. Sullivan," he said after he drained his glass. "This lemonade is so delicious, we can consider it my payment."

"It's from a Country Time mix, Greg," Grandma said. Her voice was flat. She had deep lines around her eyes. "How much do I owe?"

I saw the same look on Mr. Parker's face that I had seen on Coach Grimes'. He felt sorry for us.

"Listen. You were so good to my mother before she died. Keeping her company when I had to go to work. You do so much good for people, Mrs. Sullivan. You know you do."

Dirty Harry lay at my feet, napping in the evening heat. I scratched him on the back of the neck and pretended I wasn't eavesdropping.

"I never could thank you enough for being there for us when Mom was sick," Mr. Parker said. "Don't worry about what we've done here. The church is helping with the cost.

It's nothing much anyway."

There were truckloads of lumber and tons of nails that went into building up the front of our house. All of the shingles for the roof. The new windows. I knew what Grandma was thinking. No way was it nothing much.

The porch supports and overhang rotted because of a leak in the front part of the roof. That was why it collapsed. Mr. Parker didn't see any sign of rot anywhere else, but there were a few other areas around the house that would need patching before the end of summer. Grandma nodded while he told her this as though she meant to get it fixed right away. The negative balance I had seen on Grandma's bank statement flashed in my mind, the exact numbers tattooed into my brain.

"You will need to attend to these repairs." Mr. Parker strode across the lawn and handed his clipboard to me. Part of the floor needed to be ripped out and replaced in the kitchen and the lock on the sliding glass door was broken. There were a dozen jobs and I didn't even know how to start a single one.

I played the same game as Grandma. I nodded while Mr. Parker was talking as though I had a clue about what to do about any of it.

Mr. Parker told us to give him a call if we needed any help. Grandma smiled and walked him to his truck. I knew she wouldn't call. It was killing her to take the help she already had. When they got to the edge of the lawn she slipped him a roll of bills. He tried to push it back to her like it was hot to the touch.

"Take it," she said. "I know it doesn't begin to cover the expense. But at least it's something."

The neat roll of money rested in his open palm. He looked at it like it was a big turd that had just landed in his hand. "I'm just going to give it back to the church, Mrs. Sullivan," he said. "I told you not to worry about it."

Where she got all of that cash from, I

did not know. If he was offering to return it she should have kept it. We needed it.

"Do what you will," she said. Mr. Parker frowned. I could have told him not to argue. She was smiling, but I knew Iron Grandma when I saw her. She was not going to let him leave without the money.

He shook his head and got into his truck. After he left, Grandma passed me as she went back into the house. "Where did that money come from?" I asked.

She closed the door as though she hadn't heard me.

The sun was setting and the sky glowed pink and purple. Somebody was barbequing in a backyard somewhere. The smell made me hungry and full of memories about when Grandpa used to barbeque hamburgers in the summer. I didn't want to go back inside yet. Grandma wasn't going to talk to me anyway. Who knows how she got the money? She could have been robbing banks for all I knew.

The house smelled like new wood and paint. From the sidewalk it looked nice. Paint caked under my fingernails and splattered my shirt. I felt proud when I looked at our house. A good number of the nails in the beams were hammered in by me. I had done most of the painting.

A bicycle bell jangled and Cassie Bale turned the corner on her bike, her long hair flying like a flag. She braked when she saw me so she could roll up on the sidewalk by my side.

"Hey," she said.

I looked down at my raggedy shorts and shirt. I hadn't showered yet. White paint dotted the hairs on my arms and legs like a dusting of snow. I opened my mouth to explain everything and then closed it. There was too much. I didn't know where to start.

The pink light of the sky reflected on her face. She wore a long white tank top and shorts. She was the prettiest girl I ever saw in my life when she was just walking down the halls of school. In the warm evening she looked like a movie star or an angel.

She tilted her head. She smelled like flowers and coconut. "You look different, Matt," she said.

"I do?"

She inched closer. "Yeah. You lost weight or something."

"I guess so," I said. I had been too busy to notice. But now that she mentioned it, the shorts I was wearing used to be tight and now they were too big. They sagged even with a belt. If Grandma didn't have so much on her mind she would have told me to pull them up. She didn't abide sagging. She wouldn't care that I couldn't help it.

"I've missed you," she said.

"Really?" I thought about Mike's party. I couldn't help it. "I thought you said I was gross."

"I never said that," she said. "Who told

149

you I said that?"

I shrugged. I wasn't going to bring it up again. To tell the truth, it seemed to me like it had happened to a different person anyway. The last day of school was only a few weeks in the past, but it felt like a much longer time ago.

"Matty," she said, leaning over her handlebars. She had a tone to her voice like she had a good joke to tell me. "Come here."

I leaned in. She pulled my shirt and kissed me on the mouth.

Her lips were soft and sweet and greasy with strawberry lip gloss. A piece of her hair brushed against my face and it seemed like in that one pink-colored second everything in the world was awesome. My stomach jumped so bad it hurt. I had to force myself not to breathe hard. Panting in her face like a pervert would not be sexy. She ended that kiss with another shorter kiss and then smiled. We were so close that it looked like she had three eyes.

"Thank you," I said. Like a dummy.

"I have to get home before dark," she said. "Call me later." I watched her go, not knowing what to say, not wanting the bit of her spit that was still on my lips to dry.

She passed a strange car in the street coming towards my house. It came up our driveway. A man got out that I almost didn't recognize, but then I did, and my strange life suddenly got even stranger.

"That your girlfriend, Matty?" the man said. He didn't wait for an answer, but went right on into the house without knocking.

My dad had come to visit.

11

Manly Money

Dad and Grandma sat in front of the television and ate cake like nothing was happening. Like Dad wasn't gone for over a year. Like this was something they did every day.

Like there was no money missing from the bank account.

He sat in my place beside Grandma. She wasn't actually watching television. She was looking at him while he watched television. She watched him eat the cake like it was the most fascinating thing anybody ever did. I always said no to cake now. Maybe that hurt her feelings more than I thought.

"Isn't this wonderful, Matty?" she said. "I called your father and told him about the porch falling and he came as soon as he could."

As soon as he could just happened to be after all the work was done. I couldn't say what I was thinking.

"Come sit on the floor, son," my father said.

"I'm on the football team now," I said. I felt jacked up. I didn't want to sit on the floor.

"Is that so?"

"Yeah. Coach Grimes wanted me to, so whatever," I shrugged. I wondered if he was surprised by how much I changed. Cassie was surprised and only a few weeks had passed since I'd last seen her.

"Uh-huh," he said. He kept looking at the baseball game. He seemed very interested in the score. Maybe he would like it better if I went out for the baseball team rather than football. I couldn't tell what he was thinking.

His eyes were baggier than I remembered. His hair was shaved close to his head and he was bald on top.

"Sit down," Grandma said. "You're making us nervous hopping around."

I sat down for a second. Then I thought of Cassie and I was on my feet again.

"So that was my girlfriend out there, to answer your question," I said.

"Who? What girlfriend?" Grandma said.

"Matty was making out with a hot chick out on the sidewalk a minute ago." Dad smiled at the screen. "That's my boy."

"Who was it?" Grandma went to the new window to check it out.

"She's gone now, Grandma," I said. Cassie's perfume was still on my shirt. The game went to commercial. My dad sank back into the couch. He looked at his cell.

"Tell me it isn't that Cassie," Grandma said. She went to pour a glass of milk for my dad. Some spilled as she slammed the door of the refrigerator closed with her hip.

"Let him alone, Ma," Dad said. "Can't you tell the man is in love?" He was making fun of me but I didn't care. I couldn't care. My lips could still feel the pressure of her lips. I bounced on my toes.

Grandma made a sound through her teeth like she didn't believe in love.

"It *is* Cassie," I said. "But she's nice, Grandma. You'll see."

If Cassie could have dinner with us sometime then Grandma would have a chance to get to know her. I wondered what Cassie would think of Grandpa. Sometimes he was a mess.

"I'll *bet* she's nice." Dad smiled out of one side of his mouth. Something about the way he talked made me wish he hadn't seen us kissing.

"Matty, sit down," Grandma said.

When the game came back on, Dad leaned forward with his elbows on his knees.

He had a white milk mustache on his upper lip. I sat on the floor and asked questions about the players and the teams. Dad gave a couple of short answers until Grandma told me to be quiet. We watched him watch the game until it was over. He seemed happy with the score. He went out in back to talk on his cell for a while.

"Don't pester him with a million questions," Grandma said as we made a bed up in the guest room. She pulled up the sheet tight as a sail. "Let's not make the man tired."

"Okay," I said. "Go to bed. You're the one who's tired. I'll do this."

Grandma let go of her side of the sheet. She patted my cheek where two days before she had hit me. Her fingers brushed the spot like she wanted to wipe the slap away.

I took her hand and kissed the inside of her palm. I did that sometimes when I was a little kid. I always loved the lines in her hands for some reason. She always said her life line was long but her love line was deep.

"It's okay," I said. "Go to bed, Grandma."

After the guest room was fixed, I cleared up the cake dishes in the living room. It was dark except for the light from the television. Grandma hadn't gone to bed. She stood at the sliding glass door with her fingers on her chin, watching my father on the back patio still talking on his phone.

"Should I tell him his room is ready?" I asked. She held up her hand to tell me to be quiet. We acted the same way when Grandpa's mind cleared and he came back to us for a short while. After Grandma got mad at him on my fourteenth birthday for calling me his biggest mistake, it seemed like he was gone for good. Now we were afraid of doing or saying anything to make him leave again.

I went to my room and lay in bed. All my tiredness was gone since Cassie kissed me. I felt like I'd stuck my finger in a light socket and I was full of electricity. On top of that, I was nervous that if I did fall asleep, Dad would be gone again when I woke up.

I thought I might never sleep again.

***

Dad was there in the morning but he slept through Sunday services. During church Cassie's kiss rushed through my head and my stomach felt like an elevator crashing to the ground. I thought about Cassie during the sermon. I thought about her while the ladies presented Grandma with a plant in a blue pot to replace the one on the windowsill that got smashed when the roof fell in. I thought about her all the way home.

I wanted to see her again more than anything but I was afraid a phone call too early might break the spell. She might have already changed her mind about me and as long as I didn't call her I could still say that the last time we saw each other we kissed.

Instead when we got home I went to my room and called Mike.

"What's up?" he said.

Cassie kissed me. I almost said it. But the thought of answering any questions about what that meant stopped me.

"My dad is here," I said. "Come over for lunch after practice tomorrow." That way my dad would know that I had friends. Maybe the three of us could go to the movies or watch a game instead of me always hanging out with Mike and his dad like we used to.

"I don't think I can," he said.

"Maybe tomorrow then."

"I don't think my mom would let me," he said.

"How come she doesn't like me?" I asked. I didn't know it was going to come out like that. I always just took it for granted that Mike's mom didn't like me that much. I never thought about it before but now it just bothered me all of a sudden.

Mike didn't say anything.

"Dude," I said. The more I thought about it the more it didn't make sense. "Talk to me."

"She just wants me to have more than two friends."

"So have more than two friends."

"It's not that she doesn't like you, man. She just thinks Jester is a stoner and a drug dealer and she doesn't believe me that you're not."

"Why? I never smoked once." This wasn't totally true. I did smoke out a couple of times with Jester, but not since the beginning of freshman year. We didn't tell Mike about it. He was really straight edge about that kind of thing.

"It's not just you, Matty. Jester's selling stuff and she's freaked out."

"Jester may smoke, but he doesn't deal," I said.

Mike was quiet again.

"What?" I said. He was making me feel stupid.

"Jester *has* been dealing," he said. "Everybody knows it, man."

"How do you know? You never talk to anybody."

"Some guys in the locker room were talking about getting it with him after practice," he said.

"So you went and told your mom?" I asked. "That's so dumb, Mike."

"Not as dumb as what he's doing," he said.

I couldn't argue with that. I hadn't known Jester was selling weed, but it didn't surprise me. He was one of those guys who would do anything. He never thought about what might happen.

"But I'm nothing like Jester," I said. "I don't act the fool at your house. I'm always respectful. It doesn't make sense that your mom hates me."

161

"Look, it's not you, okay? It's your dad."

Now it was my turn to be quiet. I didn't know what to say. I didn't know what my dad had to do with Mike's mom.

"My mom knew your dad in high school," he said.

"So?" I felt weird. My skin was getting hot from the inside.

"So it isn't that she doesn't like you. Exactly. She's just afraid that you'll be like your dad was. Getting bad grades and everything. And she definitely would not let me hang out with you with him around."

"What's wrong with my dad? What do you mean like my dad was?" Now that Mike was talking smack about my dad, I felt like standing up for him.

"I don't know, man." Mike sighed. "She says he dealt weed and other stuff before he moved away. She says she doesn't trust him."

"You're saying my dad's a drug dealer

too? Because he's not. I can tell you that right now."

"Forget I said anything."

"I can't forget it. You're my best friend." I wanted to scream at Mike. "How can I be like my dad? I hardly ever see him."

Mike's mom called him away. He had to get off the phone. I wished I never called him. I was done calling people.

***

Grandma left to drive herself to a wedding to deliver one of her cakes. I think she wanted me to have some one on one time with my dad. I finished my math homework. Then I went downstairs to find him walking around the dining room in slow motion holding a sheet of yellow stickers and a notepad. He peeled away a sticker and put it on Grandma's big table that we only used for special occasions.

"I'm getting an A in Algebra," I said out of nowhere. When I was around my dad I wanted to tell him everything at once. "My teacher says she wants me to take Honors Geometry next year. I might do what she says. Math is easy for me. I'm really good at it."

I was talking too much but I couldn't help it. Dad wrote something on the sticker and then something on the notepad. I didn't think he heard me or if he did he wasn't interested.

"What are you doing?" I asked.

He looked up like he didn't know what I was doing in the house. He looked at me like I was the one who didn't belong there.

"Yard sale," he said.

"You're selling the table? Does Grandma know?"

He walked around, sticking yellow circles on the chairs. "Talk to her about it. It's decided, Matty. We'll talk when she gets home from visiting Dad."

Dad. He talked like we were brothers and not father and son.

We never had a yard sale before. Grandma liked to collect things and then sometimes give things away. She never sold anything. I couldn't believe that Grandma wanted to sell the dining table. It was from my great grandmother. Grandma kept it polished with lemon oil so it was shiny as a mirror and we weren't allowed to put glasses on it. Now Dad just stuck a big fat sticker right on the surface.

I tried calling Grandma's cell but it went to voicemail. I cinched a belt around my waist to keep my shorts up. I couldn't get it tight enough. I didn't know what to say to my dad and he was making me nervous. I went to the garage to find a nail to make another hole in my belt.

Grandpa's tools were arranged neatly on his workbench, every one of them stickered and priced.

I slid the belt from around my waist and laid it like a dead snake on Grandpa's workbench. Coach Grimes had talked to me on the sidelines before drills that morning. He asked how everything was at home. He'd heard my dad was around.

"I'll call your grandmother and see if you and she can come over for dinner some night soon," he said. It was weird. Why would I want to go to Coach's house? I wondered how much Jessica told him. He didn't say he was asking my dad over for dinner. I just shrugged and waited until he smacked my butt and let me go run drills like everybody else.

After I made the hole in my belt I went to fix a sandwich. Peanut butter and banana on wheat bread usually tasted awesome but my stomach hurt. Grandma had some new Santa statues in a row on the counter top. They had yellow stickers like the pox on their smiling brown faces.

"Sagging?" Dad came in. He tugged on

the waistband of my shorts. "Never thought Mom would allow sagging pants."

I held my shorts up with one hand and slapped down another piece of bread with the other. The belt wasn't good enough even with the extra hole. My boxers peeked out the top. They didn't fit anymore either.

My dad roamed the house with his stickers while I went back to my room to eat and read.

Tad Manly wasn't that helpful in the chapter called *Manly Money*.

A man needs money. How a man comes by his money says everything about the man. You need to work hard, yes. But you also need to work smart. You need to be paid what you are worth so that you can take care of your business. How much you need and how you make it is personal to the man. Get the degree, put in the hours. Do whatever it takes to take care of you and yours.

Just remember that money isn't everything. Far from it, in fact. Whatever you do, put your heart in it. Heart is everything.

I guess a famous NFL guy wouldn't have the kind of money problems Grandma and me had. One thing he said stuck with me though. *Do whatever it takes to take care of you and yours.*

Whatever it takes. I had to think about that.

12
Yellow Stickers

"What are you doing, Danny?"

It took Grandma a little minute once she got home to notice that my father had marked most everything in the house for sale. Her eyes were heavy. I thought that she should lie down before she did anything else but I was not about to tell her so. She was already in a delicate mood.

"It's for the yard sale, Ma," Dad said. He grabbed the apple juice out of the fridge. He started to drink it right out of the bottle but at the last second started searching around for a glass. I wondered what all he did when we

169

were out of the house besides put yellow stickers on things that didn't belong to him.

"I said *maybe* we'd have a yard sale, " she said. "I didn't say for sure. We have to talk it over some more." She had some groceries in a bag. I took it off her and put stuff away so she could sit down.

"What's there to talk about?" Dad wore shiny basketball shorts and a t-shirt. He dressed like a kid. He had a belly too. I saw where I got it from. I wondered if I was going to look the same as him when I was older. I was darker than he was but we had the same build. I hoped I wouldn't be fat. I hoped I would keep losing weight until I had six-pack abs.

Grandma didn't sit. She froze in front of the counter, staring at the Black Santas with the yellow stickers on their cheeks. Then she snapped out of it. She gathered the Santas together in one swoop so they knocked together against her chest.

"Not these," she said. She marched off to her and Grandpa's bedroom, hugging the Santas like they were her babies. She closed the door.

"She'll get over that, " Dad said. He was laughing. "I hope she's not losing her mind too."

I finished putting away the rest of the stuff from the store so that I wouldn't have to look at him and say something to get me in trouble. When I was done I noticed that I was clenching my fists.

"Come on now," he said. "I'm just kidding. It isn't funny, I know."

"You're right. It's not," I said. I didn't want to stay there with my dad but I didn't want to leave either. There were things going on that I didn't know about. I was afraid to leave and then come back and find something sold or stolen or some other way changed from the way it was before.

Dad poured another glass of juice. He

passed it to me, and told me to sit down. I stayed standing but I accepted the glass. I just held it without drinking it. I didn't drink juice anymore. *Avoid fruit juice. Eat the whole fruit instead.* Tad Manly's advice. I didn't feel like explaining it to my dad.

"I can appreciate how hard it is for you," he said. "You're just a kid who has to live with old people. That can't be easy."

"It's fine," I said. "I like living with Grandma and Grandpa. This is where I live." I took a tiny sip of juice to try to swallow down the stone of anger in my throat.

"Okay," Dad said. He held up his hands like I was trying to go off on him.

"Grandma's not even that old," I said.

"Okay," Dad said. I could tell he was laughing at me.

I thought of what Mike's mom had said about my dad selling drugs in high school. There had to be something I could say that would knock the smirk off his face.

"Did you ever get in trouble when you were my age?" I asked. "Did you sell weed or whatever?"

"That's off topic, but okay," he said. My attempt to make him get serious wasn't working. He was holding in a big old laugh. "Why do you ask? Are you in any trouble?"

"No," I said. "I told you I'm on the football team now." Part of being on the team was signing a behavior contract. Grimes lectured us every day about being men of honor. Getting caught with weed or alcohol or anything else would get us kicked off the team for good.

"Kyle Grimes still the coach?"

"Coach Grimes. Yeah." Dad wasn't answering my question about his own high school past.

He snorted out his nose like Coach was a joke too. "He's a piece of work. Maybe I'll see him before I leave."

"When's that going to be?" I asked.

"Not for a little while," he said. "Don't worry. I'm sticking around."

For the first time, that wasn't the answer I wanted to hear.

He thumbed a yellow sticker on Grandma's new blue pot that held the fern on the windowsill. When the church ladies gave it to her one of them made a speech about how much Grandma helped people. The whole church stood and clapped for her like she was a star. Grandma stood in front and patted her hair and smiled at everybody and looked happy for a minute.

I pulled the sticker off. I didn't care what he said. Grandma's fern was not for sale.

"You never answered my question," I said.

"About what?" He wiped his hand over his face. I knew he only pretended to forget.

"Did you ever do bad stuff when you were my age?"

"Did Grimes tell you that?"

"No. I just want you to tell me about you when you were a kid. This has nothing to do with Coach. He didn't say anything about you."

"I'll bet that's just what he did," Dad said. "I'll bet he badmouths me to my own kid. I'm not around to defend myself. What am I going to do about it?"

Talking to Dad was like trying to squeeze pudding. But the more he didn't answer my question, the more I needed to know the answer. "It was a long time ago," I said. "Nobody cares anymore. I just want to know."

It wasn't true nobody cared anymore. Mike's mother cared. I cared. I hated to lie but I needed the truth. I was sick of not knowing what was going on in my own life. I needed to know about my dad. I needed to know why he didn't live with us, why he stayed away so long.

I needed to know why he took all that money from my grandparents' account.

"It *was* a long ass time ago," he said. He wouldn't look me in the eyes. His mouth got soft like he had a mouthful of oatmeal. "Me and my friend dealt weed here and there. I never got caught or anything."

"Why did you do it?"

"Why? For the weed, I guess. And the money. I made a lot of money. There was no harm in it no matter what Grimes may tell you. It was better than working at fast food." He poured a glass of milk with the refrigerator door open. He was constantly thirsty. He wasn't even home twenty-four hours and Grandma already had to make an extra run to the grocery store.

"Right," I said. Now that I'd heard it from his mouth, it didn't seem that dramatic. So he sold some weed while he was in high school. So what.

"Don't tell Mom I told you, okay?" he said. He rubbed the milk mustache off on his sleeve.

"Does she know?"

He shrugged. "I don't know, man. She might. But I don't think she'd want me telling you about it."

He stuck another yellow dot on Grandma's plant, the one the church ladies gave her. He left his empty glass on the table and shuffled out of the kitchen. I peeled the sticker off as soon as he was gone.

***

Dirty Harry needed more exercise to keep him from barking at night, but it was too hot to walk him again when I got home from football. I looked online for how to take care of dogs and it turned out that a long-haired dog like Dirty Harry could get overheated in the middle of the day. We went next door for a swim in Mr. Manlow's pool. He liked it when I threw a ball in and made him fetch it. I skimmed the leaves from the surface while he paddled around.

Grandma said she'd take me to the hospital after dinner to see Grandpa and Mr. Manlow. I wanted to know if there was more I could do for Mr. Manlow. Maybe I could clean his house or something. I still felt bad about not going in to see him the morning he got hurt. I didn't feel like just telling him I was sorry because I was pretty sure he would forgive me if I asked him to. I just wanted to do more for the guy. I owed him. Plus, the more Dad hung around, the more I wanted to prove that I was different from him. I took care of people who needed me. I was really mad at him for trying to sell Grandma's stuff. What did he need the money for? If he sold the furniture, what were we supposed to sit on and eat off of? Draining my grandparents' checking and savings accounts should have been more than enough. He needed to leave us alone.

I kept skimming leaves. There was only another week left to go of summer school. I never missed a single day of class. I was proud of that. I didn't want to be the kind of person that missed school for no reason. It seemed like that was something my dad would do.

I put away the pool net. The top of my house popped up over Mr. Manlow's fence. It was where my problems lived.

"Come on," I said to the dog. He climbed up the steps out of the pool and shook. The water droplets made a rainbow. He wagged his tail as he followed me through the gate between our fences.

***

Grandma and Dad sat together at the kitchen table looking over papers. Grandma's face was tight. Dad patted her hand. "It's okay, Mom," he said. "It's for the best."

For the best? Nobody talked like that except on television when somebody was about to get screwed over. There was something wrong going on.

"Sit down, son," he said. He motioned to a chair. I wanted to stand. I hated it when he called me "son." Mike's dad always just called him Mike. I was getting madder and madder. I didn't need anybody calling me son.

"What's going on, Grandma?" I asked. Her hands were shaking.

"This is what it is, Matty," Dad said. "You're going to come live with me for a while, okay? Mom and Dad are going to live in a nice place where there are people who can take care of Dad."

"Don't talk to me like a damn baby. We take care of Grandpa," I said. "I don't want to live with you."

"You don't mean that."

"Yes I do." I tried to catch my father's eyes but he turned his head. My heart was beating a million times a minute. I expected for Grandma to hit me again or for Dad to start yelling but none of that happened. There was no drama. Dad just made a sound like he was disgusted and left the table. He went outside to his car. Grandma and I listened as he started the engine.

"Maybe he won't come back. Maybe he'll stay away forever," I said.

"He's my son," Grandma whispered. "Don't say that." She was very sad. I knelt in front of her so I could wrap my arms around her waist. I pressed my face into her hip.

"Don't send me away, " I said. "We can take care of Grandpa together, you know we can."

"It's too much for me. Your grandfather, the house." She twisted my hair, which was getting long and kind of scraggly. "The house falling is apart, Matty. We have to sell it."

"Sell the house?" I could hardly talk.

"We'll need to pay for the convalescent home for Grandpa and your dad will need the rest of the money from the sale to take care of you."

I stood up. "Wait a minute," I said. "You're planning to give your money to my dad?"

"Half of it," she said. "We should do pretty well. We paid off the mortgage before you were born. The neighborhood is good even if the house does need a fix-up. The realtor says people like living near downtown." She blew her nose. "That's all there is to it. There is no reason to make things harder than they have to be." Her eyes were red. She had been crying. My dad was the only one who ever made her cry.

"You know we don't need to do this," I said.

"Don't you see, Matty? I can't do this on my own anymore." It was like she was deaf and couldn't hear me. She had made up her mind and nothing I could say would make any difference.

"You're not on your own. You have

me."

"You're just a boy." She got up. She wiped down the counter and squirted some soap on a sponge for Dad's dirty dishes. "You need to have some time to get to know your father. A boy doesn't need to be concerned with taking care of old people and a house."

It never bothered anyone before that I lived with old people. I had lived with my grandparents my entire life. When it was convenient for my father to have his parents take care of me he didn't mind that I spent all my time with old people.

My stomach hurt. I couldn't go live with somebody who didn't care that I was in football or that I was good in math. Every time I talked to my dad I was just a pest getting in his way.

Maybe he just wanted the money Grandma would give him. He'd go waste it on whatever and I'd end up having nothing to eat except crackers for dinner. I looked down at the new pair of athletic shoes Grandma bought me for running. Dad would never spend that kind of money on me. With him I'd end up having to wear shoeboxes on my feet.

It was impossible to make Grandma understand. She wouldn't listen. She couldn't hear anything bad about my dad.

"But my friends are here," I said. "And school and Coach Grimes. The football team."

"There will be a school and football in San Francisco." She kept her back to me.

"You think he'll take care of me?" I said. "He can barely take care of himself. We have no idea what he spends money on."

"I believe that he'll grow up once you move in with him," she said. She sounded small. "If I didn't believe that I wouldn't agree to it."

"Won't you miss me?" I asked. And then I was crying like a baby. I was going to have a hard time convincing her now that I wasn't a little boy. But I couldn't move away from

Grandma. The idea of leaving my grandparents just about killed me.

She braced her hands against the edge of the counter and looked down into the sink without answering.

"How much do we need?" I asked. "How much money would make you not do this?"

"Matty," she whispered. "Don't make this hard."

"How much?"

"Stop," she said. "It's not just the money. He is your father. Don't you understand? He is finally ready to step up and be a man and look after his son. I'm not going to let him believe I don't think he can do it."

"What if he can't?"

"I have to believe that he can," Grandma said.

The word *believe* was worse than a curse word out of my grandmother's mouth. It was more important to Grandma to believe than to face facts. Grandma believed in my dad while our whole lives fell down on our heads.

I stopped arguing. I gave her a quick hug and kissed her cheek and then left the house.

But I wasn't running away. I wasn't like my dad. I was nothing like my dad.

I was going to find a way to solve our problems.

13

The Truth About Cassie

The afternoon wasn't too hot. A cool
breeze made it okay to ride around a while
without dying of heat stroke. I rode my bike
with no hands and tried texting Cassie. It felt
good to be out riding my bike. I pictured how
great it would be if she was riding next to me. I
wanted her to meet up with me and then
maybe we could go swimming after.

   She wasn't answering my texts. I didn't
feel like calling and leaving a voicemail. I wasn't
sure what my voice would do if I tried to talk to
her. I might get nervous and paralyzed and
forget how to talk. I might sound stupid. I got a

queasy feeling that Cassie wasn't my girlfriend after all. I never kissed any girls before. I didn't know what the rules were after you kissed somebody. I did know that I wanted to see her and hopefully kiss her some more.

But she wasn't answering my texts. I told myself not to worry about it. I told myself to be cool. She came to *my* house the night before and *she* kissed *me*. Cassie was the only good thing going on in my life. I didn't want to blow it by sending her five million texts in one day. Maybe she was with her parents or something and couldn't get back to me.

Skaters swarmed the bowl at the skateboard park. Jester was in the middle of everything catching air and doing crazy tricks. I could never keep my balance on a skateboard. One of the things I always liked about Jester was how he could make it look so easy. I straddled my bike and watched him for a while. I got to thinking that another thing I'd always liked about Jester was that he could take care of himself. His mom and dad split up when he was in third grade and he lived in the same house with his dad. His dad did nothing for him. Jester did everything for himself. He had to buy his own groceries and cook his own dinner. He always had plenty of cash on hand. It never occurred to me before to ask him why he always had a pocket of dollars. For some reason I always assumed that he did odd jobs for neighbors but that didn't make sense now that I thought about it.

"Hey," he said, rolling over to me.

"Hey."

We walked to the 7-Eleven. I wanted a Slurpee more than I wanted life but I forced myself to buy a bottle of water instead. It was seriously a painful choice. I didn't stick around in there too long even though it was nice and cool in the air conditioning or else I knew I'd go back on it. No man's willpower is that strong.

I paid for both of us from a five Grandma left on my dresser. I had a few things to ask and I wanted to show that we were on good terms again.

"Can we go to your house?" Jester asked.

"Bad idea," I said. "Seriously. My dad's home."

"So?"

"He's an asshole," I said. But even as I said it I felt like I was being a traitor. Even with everything happening, I felt like there was something wrong with me for talking bad about my own dad.

"That sucks," Jester said.

"I know. He wants me to move with him to San Francisco." We walked back to the park and watched this one girl in a baseball cap do a bunch of crazy tricks. There's something about a girl on a skateboard I always liked. I couldn't skateboard if my life depended on it, which made it that much more amazing to me when somebody else could do those tricks.

"You're moving?" Jester asked. "You can't move away."

I was glad that he said that. After what Mike said about his mom I wondered if I had any friends that could be seen with me.

"Seriously, Matty. You can't move."

"I know." The girl caught a bunch of air, did a turn and swooped back down into the bowl. "Especially now that I'm with Cassie."

"You're with Cassie?" he said. He looked at me over is sunglasses. The concerned friend was gone now. He was laughing his ass off.

"Yeah, man. She came over to my house last night. We totally made out."

"Oh man," he said, laughing behind his hand like I was the funniest thing he had ever seen in his life. It was pissing me off. I should have known it would be a mistake to say anything to Jester.

The girl on the skateboard looked over at us. She shaded her eyes with one hand and took off her hat with the other. It was Jessica Grimes. That was a surprise. I got the funny feeling in my stomach again. She waved at us with a big old smile on her face. I waved back but I was too pissed at Jester to look happy.

"You can't really think Cassie is your girlfriend," he said.

"Shut up," I said. "Not everything is a big joke."

"Naw, but this is. Dude." He slapped his board down and rolled towards the street. "Come with me."

***

Branches whipped me in the face. Jester pushed through the bushes ahead without thinking about what was happening to me behind him. I cursed when a switch flicked me in the eyeball. Jester told me to hush.

We hunkered down like Army guys so that no one could see us. A huge group of kids from school spread out on the sandy beach by the river. George and Jack from the football team played Frisbee in the water. Jack hollered and dove for a Frisbee. A couple of girls screamed when he splashed them. One of those girls was Cassie.

I started to get up to go see her but Jester held me back with his arm. "Wait," he said. I did what he said but it didn't feel great crawling around in the bushes like a stalker.

Cassie splashed Jack and then he ran up and grabbed her and pulled her down into the water. You would think that would make her mad but she didn't look mad. She laughed and screamed and the next thing I knew she was kissing him. He was kissing her. People yelled at them to get a room. He squeezed her butt. She ran back up to the beach to get a towel. He went back to Frisbee.

"Seen enough?" Jester asked.

She got up again and ran up behind him and put a handful of sand down the back of his shorts. He chased her up the beach. More grabbing. Kissing. Butt-squeezing.

"Seen enough?" Jester asked again.

My eyes were getting dry. I wasn't blinking. I *had* seen enough but I couldn't stop watching. Flies buzzed around my ears.

Jester grabbed me so I didn't have choice to get out of there. We shimmied back on our stomachs. Bits of river clamshells and sticks got up under my shirt and scratched me but I didn't care.

At the road we pulled my bike and Jester's skateboard out of their hiding place in a bunch of ivy. Jester kept looking at me but I didn't feel like talking about it. The weird thing was, it wasn't that big of a shock. Of course Cassie was just messing around with me. Of course she wasn't serious. I was Fatty Matty who couldn't even get up the guts to call her on the phone.

My shorts may have been too loose, and my running times may have been getting faster on the football field but none of it mattered. Cassie didn't care about me. I was going to have to move away anyway and live with my dad who I barely knew. All of my hard work was for nothing. I pumped the pedals as hard as I could. I raced forward on the trail a ways and then stopped to wait for Jester. I needed a few seconds to think.

"Are you okay, Matty?" Jester wasn't laughing anymore when he caught up.

"Yeah."

"Forget her, man," Jester said. "She's a bitch. Everybody knows it."

I looked at Jester and felt glad he was with me. Nobody else cared enough to tell me the truth.

"Dude," he said. "Why are you looking at me like that?"

"Come on," I said. "I have to talk to you about some stuff."

I got off my bike to walk it so we could talk a while in private. I was starting to think of a plan, if it could be called a plan. It was more like a desperation move. Anything was better than living away from Grandma and Grandpa. Anything was better than spending another second of my life hoping for good things to happen and then having bad things come down on us one after the other. The image of Cassie standing on the sidewalk after kissing me, her hair blowing gently in the warm breeze faded in my brain. My heart felt sore in my chest and I pictured it growing a hard shell. I was tired of feeling. I never wanted to feel anything ever again.

14
A Man With A Plan

It had been a while since I'd been to Jester's house. I didn't know why he felt like he needed to say anything about our rain gutters on our roof. His house looked ten times worse than mine ever did. The paint was peeling in curly sheets and the lawn was overgrown with weeds. At least I remembered to mow the lawn once a week. Sometimes I forgot, but I never let it get like Jester's. His was like a jungle. It made me want to take care of our front yard first thing when I got home. I didn't want people to look at our house and think bad things. Walking up to Jester's house, it seemed like either nobody lived there or freaky people lived there.

The inside smelled moldy. The television blared in the family room and his dad sat in a lumpy chair in front of it. We passed through without saying hello and went straight to Jester's bedroom.

I sat on the corner of his bed. He went swimming through his closet and pulled out a backpack from beneath a pile of shoes and dirty clothes.

"I don't usually show people this," Jester said. "I swear to God if you tell anybody I'll mess you up."

He looked over his shoulder like he was afraid somebody was listening or coming in. There was nobody around but his dad and he wasn't interested in what we were doing. The television noise was loud even from down the hall. Jester kicked the door shut. He unzipped the backpack. Instead of books it was full of money. Rolls of dollar bills wrapped in rubber bands bulged out the sides of it.

It felt like the time I got the wind knocked out of me at practice. I was paralyzed. All I could do was stare. He took out a roll to pass back and forth between his hands like a ball.

"How much?" I asked.

"You don't want to know," he said. But I did. I tried to eyeball it but it was impossible to tell. Some were twenties. Some were fives and ones. It had to be hundreds added up. Maybe thousands.

"Not all of it is mine. I owe some of it to this dude I know, Alex."

He zipped the money back in the backpack. He buried it under the junk in his closet before he grabbed a gym bag from beside his bed.

"Are you sure you want to do this?" Jester asked, being serious for once.

"Yeah," I said. Somebody had to stand up for Grandma and Grandpa. Nobody at an old folks' home would know how to take care of Grandpa right. I tried not to think about the day he walked away while I was supposed to be watching him. The truth was I could take better care of Grandpa than a bunch of strangers, and Grandma could take care of me better than Dad. Grandma and I were the only ones who could make Grandpa happy. They were the only ones who could make me happy. As far as living with Dad in San Francisco, there was no way I was going to let that happen.

"I'm okay with you being the team connection," Jester said. "Just let the players know to go to you. It makes more sense anyway. Why would I hang around at football practice? Coach Grimes would never suspect you."

"Coach Grimes?"

"Yeah. You can just pass it along in the locker room. After you whip each other with wet towels or whatever it is you do in there." He put up his hands. "I don't want to know."

"What if Coach finds out?"

"Duh. Make sure he doesn't."

Coach Grimes always told me that I could handle it when I got wiped out on the field or when I thought I could not do one more rep in the weight room. Coach Grimes came and brought us lunch the day we were building up the porch of my house. Coach Grimes helped us look for Grandpa when he got away. Jessica and Mrs. Grimes sat with Grandma and kept her calm until we found him.

I really didn't want to let him down.

"Start with that." Jester threw me the ratty gym bag filled with packages wrapped in plastic. "Sometimes there are people hanging around practice who will be looking for it. I'll let them know it's you. That whole football field area will be your territory."

"Why are you doing this for me?" I asked. Part of me wanted to talk him out of bringing me into it. "Doesn't this mean less money for you?"

"I've got more territory than I need. Just don't go beyond that. If you do I'll mess you up."

"You've got territories?" I asked. I couldn't tell if he was joking or not. It was weird to talk about drug territories. It was like we went from regular guys to Scarface in one day. Although I guess for Jester this was nothing new.

"I thought you knew I was selling," Jester said. "I've got more business than I can handle at this point, to be honest."

"Really?" The way Jester talked, he kept the whole town supplied.

"Yeah," he said. "I'm only one guy. Can't be all things to all people."

The plastic bags were mushy when I squeezed them. I had told Mike that I wasn't the same as Jester and my dad, but maybe I was.

"You don't have to do it, man," Jester said. "But I'd be a lot happier working with you than the guy I been running with lately. Dude's crazy."

"Yeah?"

"Yeah. I trust you. But you don't have to do it."

"I do have to," I said. I wanted wads of cash too. With that kind of money, I could make Dad go away. I could pay him off. I could pay for repairs to the house. I could make it so I never had to come home to find Grandma crying again.

Maybe I couldn't make Cassie Bale love me, but I could do something about the rest of my life. I zipped up the bag. I was ready to get out of there. Jester's house stank like old cooking oil and pee.

"Wait," Jester said. He went to his top dresser drawer for a lighter and a water pipe. He tossed me the lighter.

"I don't really—" I started to say.

"Just so you can say it's good shit," Jester said. He prepared the bong and passed it.

"I'm in training." I said. "Football. I'm not supposed to mess around." The smell of it was tempting. I'm not going to lie and say I didn't enjoy getting high the few times Jester and I did it before.

"You've had a bad day," Jester said. His hair flopped into his eyes. "Give yourself a break, man. Just this one time. You can go back to training tomorrow."

"I don't know," I said.

"Or don't. I don't care. Whatever, man," Jester said. "Make good choices."

"Can't your dad smell the smoke?" I asked.

"Dude," Jester said. He started to laugh. I wished I could think everything was funny. "Nobody cares. Nobody cares about anything."

I was jealous of Jester right then because I wanted not to care about my dad, my Grandpa, Cassie, anything. I wanted to hurry

204

up and stop caring. All caring got me was messed up.

I took a hit and waited not to care.

***

The empty sidewalks reflected the moonlight in silver paths. The night air carried the smell of the jasmine flowers out of people's yards. The flowers hid like invisible girls in the dark. I wished I could see those invisible girls.

I had smoked too much. I would definitely be able to testify that the weed in my bag was, as Jester would say, very very good shit.

The way home felt an impossibly long way to walk. Maybe I could choose to never go home and just spend the nights outside. I could sleep in people's backyards and garden sheds. Nobody would know. I would be very quiet and very neat.

Under the one tree by the skate park was

a nice place to rest. The sky spilled over with stars. The tree's white bark was smooth to touch and its leaves fluttered in the night breeze like thousands of clapping hands. I never noticed before how pretty it was. Stupid lonely tree.

A cop car rolled by the park. I flipped over to my stomach and tried to make myself as flat as the ground. My heart bumped against the grass. I didn't know whether to run or throw the bag full of weed in the trash and pretend I never saw it before in my life. So I didn't do anything but lay there.

He made one pass around then left. As soon as the car turned the corner I shouldered the gym bag and ran home as fast as I could with my light head and heavy feet. My dad's car was in the driveway.

I tried to tiptoe through the front door. I tried to be like a ninja in the dark.

My dad's door was open but his light wasn't on. The sharp smell of cigarette smoke wafted into the hall. High-pitched laughter answered my dad's rumbling voice.

I bumped against the table that held Grandma's keys by the coat rack and everything clattered to the floor. A brown-haired woman poked her head out of the guest room and scared the crap out of me. She wore my dad's bathrobe. She grinned and clutched the robe closed like I was trying to see her naked. She gave me an evil sidelong look and then disappeared back into the room and closed the door. I shivered.

"Matty," Grandma called, her voice raspy and strange. I climbed the stairs and passed her bedroom on the way to mine.

"Go to sleep, Grandma," I said. I wondered if my voice sounded strange too. I hoped that she wouldn't be able to tell I was high.

"You're in big trouble, young man," she said as I passed the door. But her heart wasn't in it. Dad was smoking in the house with the witch lady who was spending the night in his room. There wasn't too much she could say to me.

"I was out making things right," I said. "You can count on me." But my heart wasn't in it either.

15

Manly Brothers

A man needs brothers. I'm not talking about brothers you are related to necessarily. I am an only child, but I have brothers. I'm talking about men who would defend you in a fight. Men who will call you on it if you are acting the fool. My father always said to me that a man who is your friend through thick and thin is a treasure, for that man is your brother. –Tad Manly

I pressed my face into the hot muddy grass of the football field. I tried to will myself to disappear into the dirt like an earthworm in

Grandma's garden.

"Get up, Matthew," Coach yelled in my ear.

I hated Coach Grimes. I wanted him to disappear too. First him, then me. I breathed a blade of grass into my nose by mistake and sneezed.

Coach grabbed my shoulder and flipped me over. He put his fingers under my eyes and pulled down. I tried to push him away but I was too late and too weak.

"Leave me alone," I said. "I feel sick."

He peered closer. I could smell his minty gum. It was never a good day when Coach Grimes got close enough so that I could smell his minty gum. The sun blared in my eyes.

"What's wrong with you, son?" He clenched his teeth like he was mad.

It was like my first day of practice all over again. Only it was worse because at least on my first day Grimes wasn't pissed at me and I wasn't breathing through lungs filled with glue. I didn't know why he didn't just believe me that I was sick. People got sick sometimes. It happened. It was like he knew I was lying. I didn't know how but he always knew.

"What did you do?" he asked.

"Nothing," I said. "I'm just sick." Either the ground was spinning under me or the sky was spinning over me.

He sniffed at my hair. He started chewing at his gum faster. I wished I took a shower when I came in the night before but I was too tired and out of it. He narrowed his eyes and sniffed again.

He could tell. He knew I had been smoking and he knew what I was smoking.

He lifted me up by my shirt and put me on my feet. "What kind of man are you, Matthew? You get to choose. Nobody but you."

"Yes sir," I said. I tried to look away. He grabbed my ear and made me look him straight in the eyes. Pain shot through the side of my head and woke me up. I'd never seen him so mad.

"You're running," he said. He was right up in my face. "You're running until you puke, and then maybe you'll think about how bad that feels next time you want to do something stupid."

My head pounded. He smacked me on the butt. My feet felt like they weighed four tons each. I wasn't running the field any more. I didn't need this. I jogged towards the locker room, where I was going to leave my uniform and go home and never come back.

Coach called after me. "Matthew," he said. His voice was heavy with warnings and push-ups and five hundred more runs across the field. George ran over to us. Coach yelled at him to get back to work. He looked back at us over his shoulder with a worried look on his face and for some reason that made me feel worse than anything else.

But there was no point to being on the team. I put up with Coach Grimes yelling at me and making me run stairs and learn plays and I killed myself on the field every morning, and for what? Cassie was with Jack. She would never want me. If I didn't get out and sell Jester's weed hiding in my gym bag in the locker room then I wouldn't be able to stay in town long enough to see the start of the football season anyway.

Jester watched the practice from outside the chain link fence. There were a couple of guys standing around next to him. He pointed me out to them.

Coach barked my name. The sun beat down. My lungs hurt. Everything hurt.

Jester's friends leaned against the fence. I recognized them as a few of the older dudes I saw him with sometimes in the park. There was one I never saw before. He had a long black braid over a shaved head. He nodded my way as I passed by.

I couldn't look back at Coach Grimes. He knew I had been smoking weed, and he probably figured I was about to try to sell it too. He knew everything. It was stupid for Jester to come to the practice.

Maybe Grimes would call Grandma and tell her about it. Maybe he would call the police. There was nowhere safe to go. I stopped jogging and just stood there in front of the door to the locker room.

Coach came up behind me. "Those friends of yours, son?" He jerked his head towards Jester.

"No."

"Then get back out there and finish the practice."

I rested my hands on my hips and tried to catch my breath.

"You should know that it doesn't matter," I said over my shoulder. Jessica stood a ways away holding a water bottle, watching us.

He looked at me like I was speaking a language he didn't understand. "Seriously, Coach," I said. "You're wasting your time."

"What are you talking about?"

"My dad's taking me to San Francisco."

Coach scowled. "Finish the practice," he said. "It is what it is. You came to practice today. Finish what you came here to do."

I looked down the field of grass. The morning sun made it smell like a hot mowed lawn. I would never smell a mowed lawn again without thinking of football practice.

"I don't know, Coach," I said.

"Seriously, Matty. You're not gone yet. Ain't a thing set in stone yet. You never know." He talked like a fortune cookie. I had no idea what he meant.

Coach Grimes clapped his hands and called out a direction to the rest of the team.

"Matt, you run stairs," he said. Everybody else would run plays. He put his hand on my back and pushed me along like it was already

215

decided. Like I was maybe his kid.

But I wasn't his kid. Coach could look into my eyes and smell the pot smoke in my hair all he wanted. I could never be his son.

Once I left the field to sell what was in my gym bag, there would be no going back. There would be no Manly Matthew, or Grandpa's strong young man. Whoever Grimes saw as worth letting onto the team would leave the field forever and never ever come back to it.

"It is what it is," I said under my breath. I pivoted and ran towards the bleachers. I would finish what I'd come that morning to do. I would finish up one more practice for old times' sake.

"It is what it is," I said again and again. No need to get sad about it. It was what it was.

***

"I heard you have something," one of

the varsity guys said to me while I shoved my cleats into my bag.

"What?"

"Jester said to go to you," he said.

I touched the smooth plastic of the bags under the dirty socks in my bag. I'd brought half the stash with me to sell to the players.

"So do you have it or not?"

What kind of man are you going to be? You get to choose. Coach had sounded so sure. I held the weight of one of the bags in my hand but I didn't take it out.

"Meet you outside," I said. He went back down the benches to the other varsity guys. I finished putting my gear up and went out. Mike called after me but I acted like I didn't hear him.

I didn't wait to meet anybody. I shouldered my gym bag and kept walking. I left my bike on the racks to avoid Jester and his friends by the fence.

"It is what it is," I said to myself. I didn't

even know what it meant but it helped me keep walking.

"Matty!" A girl was calling my name. I knew who it was and I shouldn't have stopped but I couldn't help it. Something about Cassie had me hypnotized.

She left a group of the players' girlfriends waiting outside the school and ran up to me.

"Didn't you hear me calling you?" she asked. I shrugged and started walking again. I needed to get going before I ran into anybody else. I needed time to figure shit out.

"What's wrong?" She pulled my shirt. It was annoying.

"Nothing," I said. "What do you want?"

"Meanie," she said, skipping ahead of me and laughing. "Why are you in such a bad mood?"

"Go find Jack," I said.

"We're in a fight. I'm not even talking to him right now." She danced up to me and put her hands on my chest. I didn't want her to smell me. I was sweaty. I didn't want her to feel my fat. I pushed her away. Not hard but I wasn't playing around.

"What the hell?" she said. She sounded hurt. I wasn't ready for her to sound hurt.

I was in love with you. I clenched my teeth and bit down on everything I wanted to say. She looked up at me through her eyelashes and her lips were so pretty. The same lips she planted all over Jack on the beach.

"I saw you," I said.

"Saw me where?"

"At the river."

Then she just started talking. She was really confused. She had so many feelings. She didn't know what she wanted. That voice I used to love so much. Now it was just getting on my nerves. She saw me as somebody to mess with. I would never mean anything to her.

I walked past her. She called after me. "It is what it is," was all I could say back. Nothing else made sense anymore.

***

The skate park baked in the sun like a desert of white concrete dunes. The skaters would come out in the evenings to roll and flip their boards on the ramps and bowl but now it was hot as the sun. The one tree didn't quiver in the still air. The bottoms of my feet burned.

A row of stores in a mini mall lined the main street just past the park. They used to be a donut shop, a liquor store and a taqueria before they closed. Now the only thing that stayed open was a check cashing place with a neon sign flashing GET MONEY in the window. I turned the corner around the building and there was Jester and the guy with the braid leaning against a white Mustang with bass booming out of its stereo.

Jester jumped forward. He was waiting for me. "Dude, where'd you go?" He punched me hard on the shoulder. Something was wrong with him. He was nervous and weirder than usual.

"I had to get out of there, man," I said. "Coach wouldn't leave me alone."

Jester's friend stared at me, his arms crossed in front of his chest. I couldn't see his eyes, only my own reflection in the mirrors of his sunglasses.

"So you didn't sell nothing?" the guy said.

"Naw," I said. I took my bag off my shoulder and opened it on the sidewalk. The guy cursed.

"Are you retarded? Get in the car."

Jester was going to hop out of his skin. He opened the car door and pulled me in while his pal stood watch on the sidewalk.

"Who is that guy?" I asked.

"Alex," Jester said. "He's mad that I gave

you all this without asking him." He reached in and took out all the bags. "This is it? Where's the money?"

"I told you. Coach was all over me."

"Where's the rest of it?"

"Home."

"Jesus, Matty." He acted like I was the biggest idiot in the world. "I thought you wanted a chance to make some serious money."

"I do," I said. Sweat dripped off my nose until I wiped it with my sleeve. "Look, Jester. I don't think I can do this after all. I'll have to think of another way."

"What are you talking about?"

I don't want to be like my father. The thought screamed so loud in my brain I heard it in my ears. I shook my head. If I had a choice about what kind of man I was going to be, hunching over a bag of weed in a hot car wasn't it.

"Matty," Jester said. "I'm talking to you."

"I've got Grandma or Coach breathing down my neck all the time," I said. "I thought I could do it but I can't."

"It's not that simple," Jester said. "I should have never brought you in. Shit."

I zipped up the bag and got out on the other side. Jester followed me.

"What's going on?" Alex called over the top of his car.

"I'll bring the rest to your house later," I said to Jester. "Sorry." It had to be that simple. I couldn't sell weed even to keep my grandparents and me together. There had to be other ways to make the kind of money I needed.

Jester looked like he might cry. He rushed over to Alex. "He's cool," he said. "Don't worry, man."

But Alex ran up and punched me in the face so quick I didn't know what was happening until it happened. I hit the asphalt. Blood filled my mouth. He kicked me in the side. Pain burst in my lower back. I rolled away but he kept coming with his hard boots.

Jester just stood on the sidewalk and watched. I tried to get on my feet but Alex didn't give me time. All I could see was the side of the building, a tire, a crumpled cigarette wrapper in the gutter. He kept coming at me. I threw my arms over my head and curled into a ball.

A silver car turned the corner. Alex stopped kicking me. There was the sound of car doors slamming. The Mustang tore away, stereo roaring through the open windows. The tailpipe blew smoke. Gravel cut into the side of my face.

"You okay, young man?" The driver in the silver car was a lady with two little girls in the back seat. I forced myself to get up.

"I'm okay," I said. I clutched my side. It hurt to stand.

"Want me to call the police?"

"No," I said. "I'm okay."

"I don't think you are," she said. One of the kids in the back seat started to cry.

"I'm okay," I said again. I started for home. I guess she believed me because she drove off. The only thing I cared about was getting into the house before Alex and Jester came back. I went through the side gate and snuck upstairs to take a shower before Grandma could see me bloody.

16
A Man of His Word

A Manly man says what he means and means what he says. Don't make promises you can't keep. If you make a promise, make it happen. It only takes one broken promise or lie to undo someone's trust in you. My father always says that a true leader builds his reputation on trust, and that's built one kept promise at a time.

My father always says that a man should not do anything he is ashamed to tell the truth about to everyone he meets. That should be your test before you make any decision to speak or act. Would you be willing

*to tell the truth about it later? Would you be
proud to tell that truth?*

*A man of honor tells the truth. It's as
simple as that. If you want to be a man of
honor, keep your promises and always tell the
truth.* –Tad Manly

I stayed in my room. My cheekbone
throbbed where Alex socked me. I wouldn't let
Grandma in when she knocked.

"What's the matter?" she called through
the door.

"I just want to be left alone," I said.

"The hospital called. We can take
Grandpa home tonight," she said. The stairs
creaked as she went down them.

Just when I had Jester's drug dealer to
deal with, I was going to have to worry about
Grandpa running away. My cheek felt burning
hot. I lifted my shirt in front of the mirror.
Swollen blotches bloomed across my side and
stomach. I could barely open my right eye.

I looked at myself and felt calm despite the mess. I wasn't going to sell drugs. I wasn't going to break the law. I was the kind of man who didn't break the law. That was the kind of man I was. It felt good to have made that one decision. I was a lot of things but I wasn't a drug dealer.

I took a deep breath in and let it out even though it hurt. It would have saved me trouble if I'd made that law-abiding decision about myself sooner but it was made now. Maybe I didn't have any control over what my dad and Grandma decided for my life. Maybe I'd end up getting beat up again. At least I was in charge of myself. At least I knew that much.

I stayed in my room for a while and read the rest of *How to Be Manly*. Maybe there would be a line in there that would tell me what to do. Every couple of minutes Jester called my cell phone but I wasn't picking up.

Then somebody knocked on my bedroom door. I glanced in the mirror again.

Grandma was going to flip out. I couldn't let
her see me.

"I'm sleeping," I said.

"Matthew. Open up." It was Coach
Grimes. I shoved the book under my mattress.

"I'm sick," I said.

"In the head," he said. "Open up."

I'd buried Jester's gym bag filled with the
rest of the weed in my dirty clothes hamper in
the closet. There were no better hiding places
in my room. I unlocked the door. Coach
stepped right in, sniffing around like a hound.
The smell of Grandma's cake baking came up
from the kitchen.

He quit sniffing when he saw my face.
"What the hell happened to you?" He grabbed
my jaw and turned my head so he could see
my black eye.

"Don't worry about it," I said clenching
my jaw against the pain.

"Don't tell me not to worry about it. Was
it those boys outside the fence at practice

229

today? You in some kind of trouble?"

My cell phone buzzed on my bed. I
ignored it.

"No sir," I said. "Me and a friend were
just messing around and it got out of hand."
Grimes gave me a sidelong look like he didn't
believe me.

"It was just an accident," I said. "You do
worse to me on the field every day." I forced
myself to smile. Getting Coach involved in my
problems would just make everything worse. I
needed to figure it out on my own.

"This was no accident," he said.

Coach Grimes was a huge man. He
crowded my room. He pulled out the chair
from under my desk and sat down.

"What's this about you going to live
with your father?" he asked. "Where is he,
anyway?"

"He's around." His car wasn't in front of
the house but his stuff was still in the guest
room.

"Why is your grandmother selling the house now?" He lowered his voice like he wanted this to be just between us. Downstairs, Grandma ran the mixer.

"She says she can't handle fixing all the stuff that's wrong with it," I said.

"The church paid for fixing the porch. Your grandmother has done so much for other people through the years and we were all glad to do it. Her friends would be willing to do more, if she just asked. "

"Well, it's what my dad wants," I said. "It was his idea and she's going along with it."

"Huh." Coach looked out the window. "It doesn't make sense. You all have roots here in this community. Why move now?"

I didn't know what to say. He was asking questions for grown ups to answer. How was I supposed to know anything except what people told me? "I guess since Grandpa ran away and the porch fell in she feels like she can't handle everything by herself any more."

"She's not by herself," he said. "She has us. She has you."

The way he said it made me feel strange. He talked like I was someone grown who could take care of business.

"Listen to me, Matthew," Coach said, waving his enormous hands. "I'm going to talk to Mrs. Grimes and see what can be done about this situation. I want you to trust me."

"What can Mrs. Grimes do?"

"She's a lawyer."

I knew that Mrs. Grimes was a lawyer, but I didn't know how Coach thought she could help. Dad didn't steal Grandma's money. They had a joint account. She told him to take what he needed. It wasn't a crime to suck as a human being, unfortunately.

I did trust Coach but I couldn't see a way out of the problem without a bag full of cash. Not even Coach Grimes could get his way on everything.

"Meanwhile, I need to trust *you*," he

said. "Not to do anything stupid to break your grandmother's heart." He put a heavy hand on the back of my neck.

"Right," I said.

"I need you to promise me, Matthew. No more smoking. Do you get me?" He squeezed my muscles back there and it hurt but I didn't show it. "Whatever those boys wanted with you on the field today, those are not your friends."

My phone went off again like an angry bee. He didn't need to tell me they were not my friends. I already knew that.

"Do you get me?" he asked.

"Yeah. I get you," I said. "I promise."

We shook on it. I followed him downstairs. Grandma would have to see me sometime. It might as well be when I had Coach nearby for protection.

"Boys," she called. "Come on and have some cake."

She was waiting at the table with a cake

and two glasses of milk.

"Matty! Your eye!" She dropped the cake knife on the floor as she rushed me.

"Don't mind if I do, Mrs. Sullivan," Coach said. He picked up the knife and put it in the sink before sitting down like nothing was going on. "This is wonderful cake. What a treat."

"What happened to my grandson?" She held my face in her hands. Even her gentle touch hurt my cheekbone.

"Mrs. Sullivan, you know better than anybody that boys will be boys. He just got to playing a little rough on the field today, that's all. He'll be fine."

Then Coach started asking about the people she was baking and cooking for. The kitchen was too warm. The air conditioner couldn't compete with Grandma's oven. She looked doubtful but sighed and sat down with us. I ate some too without trying to stick it in the sink. Red velvet. The frosting stuck to the roof of my mouth like an old friend.

"The Pulidos have a new baby," she said. "So there's a casserole for them. And I'm selling the cakes, of course. Someone always has a birthday or an anniversary." She looked at me and frowned. "So did that happen to your face on the field? And why are you walking funny?"

The doorbell rang. I ran to answer it to escape Grandma but I wished I didn't. It was Jester and Alex. The cake congealed in my stomach. I wanted to throw up.

"Dude, where is it?" Jester's words were bullets. He acted like we were never friends. "You need to quit playing around."

I stepped out and closed the door. "Wait here," I said. "I'll bring it down. But then you need to leave me alone. I'm out of this." Alex's face was stone. I caught a look at myself in his sunglasses. He grabbed me by the neck of my shirt.

Just then Coach Grimes flung open the

door and came up behind me like an overgrown shadow.

"Gentlemen," he said.

Jester's eyes popped out of his head. It would have been hilarious in any other situation. Coach crossed his arms in front of his chest and looked down on them with his face hard and crazy. I never saw him look so mean in my entire life.

"Come on, man," Jester said. He pulled on Alex's arm. Alex yanked it back. He put a finger in my face.

"Give it up," he said as if Coach wasn't even there.

My bones felt cold despite the heat.

Coach stepped forward and got between Alex and me. "Back off, boy," he said. His voice was quiet but I knew then that he would defend me if it came to it. He would get in a fight for me.

Alex smirked and turned slowly like it was his idea to leave. Jester was already waiting in the car. Alex got in the driver's side and squealed the tires before zooming down the street.

"You want to explain that?" Coach asked. Now he was mad at me.

I shook my head. Grandma came out wanting to know what all the screeching tires were about.

"It's nothing," I said. "Just a misunderstanding with Jester. Don't worry about it."

"What kind of misunderstanding?" Grandma wiped her hands on her apron. "I like that boy less and less. Is he the one who gave you the shiner?"

I touched the puffiness on my face. Grimes motioned me to follow him to his truck. Grandma watched us from the porch.

"Be careful," he said. "I've got some things I have to do but I'll drop by again later to make sure everything is okay."

"Don't bother," I said. "Everything's cool."

"Whatever mess you're in, Matthew," Coach said as he got in his truck, "everything is not cool."

At that point I thought I just needed some time to figure things out. I thought that I could get out of trouble and fix the mess I made if I could just get some time to think.

Coach backed down into the street. A car with a loud stereo passed by, making me jump. It wasn't the white Mustang this time. But at some point it would be.

***

"You're a punk, Fatty Matty."

I finally picked up my phone on Jester. We needed to talk sense.

"I didn't tell Coach Grimes to come over," I said.

"I'm not playing games with you. I can't believe I trusted *you*."

"I can't believe I trusted you," I said.

"You got me in trouble with your crazy friend. What am I supposed to do now?"

"You should have just sold it," he said. "Then he'd know you're cool."

"Just take it," I said. "I don't want it anymore."

"You are such a punk. Even worse, you're making me look like a punk."

"This doesn't make any sense. It's not that big of a deal."

"The hell it isn't, Fatty. Alex is insane. And paranoid. Bring the stuff to my house right now or you bring me the money. I am not playing with you."

I wasn't playing either. There was nothing about this that was a game to me. My bruised ribs and eye turning purple felt pretty damn serious. Once Grandma left the house I'd be over with the bag if I made it there without getting jumped. He said a string of cuss words and then hung up on himself while he was still talking. It was like one of his old tricks except that it wasn't funny.

***

Grandma left to go bring cakes and dinners to people. After she made her deliveries she was going to go pick up Grandpa. I helped load it all into the back of her car, looking up and down the street to see if anybody was coming.

"Everything okay?" Grandma asked. I nodded like it was nothing but I wanted to tell her. She wiped her forehead with her sleeve and I got this tidal wave feeling in my chest. Tears came to my eyes and I couldn't stop them. I flung my arms around her neck so hard she almost fell over.

"What's this?" she said, patting my back.

"I just love you, Grandma." She smelled like vanilla and sugar.

"I love you too, Matty. We'll all be okay."

I didn't believe her. Unless she could take care of me and I could take care of her, nothing would be okay again.

***

The phone in the kitchen rang. I picked it up because I thought it would be one of Grandma's friends.

"Hello?"

"I know you're alone in the house, man."

"I'm coming by in a minute. Give me a chance."

"Stay there," he said. "We're right down the street."

"You're bringing Alex?"

Somebody was talking in the background. "You better be there," Jester said. His voice was high pitched as a girl's. He was more scared than I was.

I hung up. Maybe I should have stayed there and just handed over the bag. But something in Jester's voice made me know that Alex wouldn't just let me give him back the weed. I didn't want to hang around for that.

Since he'd been in the hospital, Grandma kept the key to Mr. Manlow's house on a little hook by our door. Dirty Harry followed me out with his head low. He understood we had to be sneaky.

Dirty Harry ran around inside his own house, checking all of the rooms. He was looking for Mr. Manlow and it was sad. I closed all the blinds.

A car drove by booming a bass line. I crouched down and peered out from two slats in the blinds. It was Alex's white Mustang. He slowed down at the corner and stopped. A bunch of dead flies dusted the windowsill under my nose. Their little black legs curled against their bodies.

The bass from the car stereo shook the windows. My chest bone vibrated. Then the motor revved up and the car and its noise drifted away.

I walked through all the rooms like the dog. Somebody rolled by outside on a skateboard.

My cell phone rested heavy and quiet in my front pocket. I didn't even notice when Jester quit calling. He used to be my friend. One of my only two friends. Now I didn't even have one. If I called Mike he wouldn't come help me. His mother wouldn't let him out of the house.

If Coach got involved then he would have to find out about the weed that I got from Jester. He would kick me off the team. I wouldn't be allowed to talk to Jessica anymore. Grandma would send me away to San Francisco for sure or maybe to one of those boot camps for bad kids that I saw on one of her talk shows. Boot camp would be easy after working out with Coach Grimes. That was my only consolation.

Alex boomed past again. I dropped to the floor. I had needed time to think. Now I had it. I was trapped.

17
Hide and Seek

Dust floated in the sunlight coming through the thin gap in the curtains. It hung in the air like stars in a tiny calm universe until I blew on it and flipped the particles around in swirls. Mr. Manlow's house was dusty as hell.

I started wiping dust off the table with a towel from the kitchen. It flew into my nose. An empty bookcase stood against the wall surrounded by boxes. Some boxes were marked BOOKS and some with a long name written in shaky black marker, THADDEUS. I unpacked the boxes and put the books up on the shelves. The job would have been impossible for Mr. Manlow with his weak hands. No wonder the boxes stayed packed. I should have offered to help him a long time ago.

I shelved books and tried to think of what to do but my mind stayed blank. It was like I was stuck on an island surrounded by dangerous waters with no way to leave.

Somebody knocked on the door of Grandma's house. I peeked out the kitchen window. Jester was on my front porch. Alone. Dad's car wasn't in the driveway. Grandma wouldn't be back for another three hours. I could give him the stuff. We could settle everything for good.

I almost ran out the back door to catch him before he left. Then I stopped for a second and listened. There was an engine idling. I dropped and crawled to the window in front. The dead flies scattered under my nose. I was breathing hard. The Mustang with Alex at the wheel sat in Mr. Manlow's driveway like a waiting shark.

"Matty, you fat ass," Jester yelled. His voice echoed in the alley between the houses. The neighbors were going to hear him. "You don't have to hide. I'm by myself. Come on out."

He turned to where Alex was watching and shrugged his shoulders. Alex backed out of Mr. Manlow's driveway. He gunned down the street and cut around the corner and was gone. He left Jester standing under the new overhang I had helped to build. I backed off from the window.

Dirty Harry stuck his nose in my ear. Then he put up his head. Outside the gate in the fence opened and slammed closed. Dirty Harry lowered his ears and growled. Jester was in the backyard. A shadow darkened the sliding glass door. He tried pulling it open. It rattled. I prayed that I had remembered to lock it.

Jester and Alex could kill me in Manlow's

house and Grandma wouldn't know where I was. They wouldn't find my dead body until Mr. Manlow was well enough to come home.

Dirty Harry exploded into crazy barking. I lay flat on the floor and kept perfectly still. The sliding door shook harder this time. It was locked but it sounded like it might break.

"Matty," the muffled voice of my former friend Jester called. I stayed down. For all I knew Alex parked and ran back, waiting somewhere ready to jump me.

"Matty, it's Jester," he hit the glass again. "I know you're in there. I can hear the dog."

Dirty Harry lunged at Jester's shadow. I got up. Maybe the dog would protect me.

"Are you alone?"

"Yeah I'm alone. Call off the dog, man. I've got to talk to you."

"You weren't alone a minute ago. Your boy was waiting for me in the driveway. I saw him."

"He left me. Open up before he comes back. Damn."

I unlocked the door and slid it open. Dirty Harry jumped on Jester as he came in. Jester threw up his hands and backed up against the wall. I grabbed the dog's collar to pull him down.

"What's wrong with him?" Jester asked, tugging at his t-shirt trying to act like he wasn't scared.

"He hates traitors and assholes," I said.

"I had no choice. Alex is about to kill me for giving you that stash. If only you sold it like you said you were going to. He's sure you're a narc or a snitch and he's about to go off on both of us."

"I said I'd give it to you," I said.

"Then why are you hiding over here?"

"I'll give you the bag right now," I said. "But then I want you and Alex to leave me alone. We'll pretend it never happened okay?"

Jester rubbed the side of his face with

one hand. He was sweating. "You're in it now, Matty. You can't get away that easy."

"Then what?" I asked. Jester and his friend were like something nasty stuck to my finger that I couldn't shake off no matter how hard I tried. "I'm not a narc, I'm not interested in your business. It was a mistake. I thought I could do what you do but I can't. Nothing is worth that to me."

"Worth what?" Jester frowned.

"Worth everybody thinking I'm a loser," I said.

"Who thinks I'm a loser?" Jester stopped hopping around and looked at me as though I had said something truly puzzling. Like I had just given him brand new information.

"Everybody." Dirty Harry whined as I raised my voice. I didn't care. "Everybody thinks you're a loser. Do you think you're getting away with anything? You're not. Everybody knows what you do, Jester. Pretty soon you're going to get caught and then you'll have to go to Juvenile Hall or whatever. Boot camp."

Jester looked down and shrugged. "I've got to make money. Weed is no worse than beer. Pretty soon it will be legal anyway."

"Wake up, Jester," I said. I felt like I was the grown up and he was a dumb kid. I couldn't believe that the day before I was trying to be just like him. "Did you know that Mike's mom doesn't let him talk to us anymore? Did you even know that? She doesn't allow us over to the house. At next year's end of the year party, you and I will not be invited."

"Why?" he asked. His eyebrows were raised. He hand to God had no idea what I was talking about.

"Because you're always acting like a lunatic," I said. "You're famous for it, if you want to know the truth."

He halfway grinned at that. "So? She lets me come over."

"When was the last time you hung out with Mike?"

"The pool party," he said. His smile disappeared. "I've been kind of busy, actually. I haven't even called Mike since then."

"You should try it," I said. "Because the days of the three of us going over there and playing X-Box are over. She hates us. Mike told me." I didn't care if I hurt Jester's feelings. I wanted to hurt them. I wanted him to see what was really going on.

"But why you?" Jester said. "Why should she hate you? You didn't do anything." He picked up a ceramic football trophy from the shelf and looked at it. I took it away and put it back.

"Because I hang out with you, for one thing. And since my dad is in town, she won't let me near Mike. I guess my dad used to sell too. Still does I guess." I hated even saying it out loud but now that I did I knew it was true.

"So?" Jester said. Nothing I was saying

was sinking in. A car with a loud engine started up the street. I pulled Jester down and peeked out the window. Alex drove with one hand on the steering, head bent low to peer around.

Jester cursed in a harsh whisper. He smelled like metal. I looked at the side of his face.

"You're scared," I said.

"He's really pissed." Jester said. His shoulders hung forward and his chest was sunken in. He was so skinny. I thought of his dad sitting in front of the television. I tried to remember the last time we had Jester over for dinner. "Look, I'm sorry that Alex jumped you today," he said. "And I'm sorry I got you in this. Alex is crazy. One reason why I was glad you wanted in with me is because I'm sick of dealing with that loco by myself."

"How do I get out?"

"Dude. There might be one thing you can do to get out of it, and it would be a favor to me."

"Look," I said, trying one last time. "This sounds weird but I'm trying to be better than my dad. Do you have any idea what I mean by that?"

Jester kept his eyes on the street through the crack between the curtains. "Remember when we were in sixth grade and those two eighth grader guys started picking on Mike for no reason?"

I did remember. They stole his glasses and Mike had to tell his parents what happened. They came down to the school and the boys got in trouble with the principal, which just made life worse for Mike after. People called him a snitch, which was the worst thing anybody could ever call you.

Then all of a sudden the guys left Mike alone. One day he couldn't even go to the bathroom without getting jumped and then the next, the two guys who were bugging him just faded away and never looked at him again.

The familiar growling engine passed by

again. The windows vibrated with the bass coming out of his speakers. I wondered how many times he planned to circle the block. Jester stretched out on the carpet and rested his hands on his chest.

"There's something I never told you," he said. "I never told anybody this."

He was still for once, just looking at the ceiling like it was the most interesting thing in the world. I waited for him to talk.

"Do you remember that bonehead Del hung out with?" He asked. I nodded. I didn't remember his name, but the guy who was Del's partner in crime was a quiet guy, leaner than Del but just as mean. Both of them together were bad news to Mike.

"I found out where that guy lived. I went to his house one night and I snuck in through his window. I carried my dad's hunting knife in my teeth like a ninja. You should have seen me."

I pictured Jester climbing into a

stranger's window in the middle of the night with a knife in his mouth. As crazy as it sounded I believed him.

"He was dead asleep. I pressed it into to his neck. Then I whispered in his ear to wake up." Jester had a dreamy look on his face. "He opened his eyes and he jumped a little, you know? Like I scared him. I cut him right under the chin. His eyes were about to pop out of his head. He started crying like he was about to die."

"Shit, Jester."

"I told him they better leave Mike alone or I'd come back when he didn't expect it and kill him in his sleep. I think the guy wet his bed. It was hilarious."

"Why him and not Del?"

"Del was like Alex. He wouldn't care if I cut him. But his punk friend was scared. The very next day they ignored Mike totally. He got Del interested in something else I guess. I don't know how he did it. I don't care. But he never bothered my friend again."

I rubbed Dirty Harry under his neck.

"I don't care if you believe me," Jester said. "What I just told you is true."

"I believe you," I said.

"So you can't say I'm a bad friend. I was just trying to help you. I make a lot of money, you know? But I didn't think it through. Sometimes I do things without thinking."

"Really?"

Jester half-smiled. He was strangely calm. Not jumpy or sweating anymore. Talking about being a ninja made him feel great.

In junior high Mike had been getting threats and socks in the stomach and all kinds of hassle every day at school. It was to the point that he started missing a lot of days. Nothing his parents or teachers did made any difference. Only Jester was willing to do what it took. He was the only one crazy enough to face down the crazy.

All of the times when we spent the night

at Mike's house or when Grandma took us to ice cream seemed like a hundred years ago. Even Mike's end-of-the-year party seemed to have happened in another time when we were kids.

Jester got up. "Come with us tonight to meet this guy we're selling to. Then you'll be done with it."

"Us?"

"Me and Alex."

"Why would I do that? Alex wants to kill me."

Jester shook his head. "Not if you come with us tonight. There might be something funny about this meet up we're doing. I've never met the guy before."

"Who is it? Does he go to our school?"

"Naw. He's older. Alex sold to him before but he doesn't trust him for some reason."

"Does Alex trust anyone?"

"I have no idea. It's a huge deal. He wants back-up and you're it." He made for the door. "Come to my house with the weed at nine. We'll go from there."

"Alex is going to kill me," I said. The facts hadn't changed. I couldn't trust what either Jester or Alex would do.

"Naw," Jester said. "After this he'll leave you alone, I promise. Just come with us to meet this guy who's supposed to buy us out tonight. I'll even give you a percentage. Okay?"

He held out his hand for me to shake. I took it and his hand was dry. He saluted me with his other hand and slipped out the back door. Dirty Harry growled and barked once more and then Jester was gone.

18

The Man on the Driver's Side

Back in my own house, Dad was home. His backside hung out the refrigerator.

"Mom keep any barbeque sauce around?" he asked.

"She makes her own recipe," I said. It was weird to have to tell him something like that about his own mother. He scratched the back of his head.

"Oh yeah. Forgot about that." He smiled. "Man, she can cook. And bake. Nobody better, that's for sure."

"You cook for a living," I said. "You're probably great." I hated myself for being nice to him but I couldn't help it. Part of me still wanted my dad to like me.

"I pass good enough," he said, still smiling like we were in on a joke together. I didn't know what the joke was and I felt like a fool. "What happened to your eye?"

"Long story," I said. I had four hours until I had to meet Jester. I didn't know whether to feel nervous about the meet up or relieved that Alex wasn't cruising by the house anymore.

"It looks bad," he said. "Whoever it was I hope you kicked his ass."

"You should cook for us tonight," I said, turning away from him. It wasn't good to curse in Grandma's house. "To celebrate Grandpa coming home."

"He's coming home tonight?" His smile fell away. "Seriously?"

"Yeah, seriously," I said. "What kinds of things do you make at your restaurant?" I didn't even know the name of the place where he worked.

He rubbed his hands together, cheering up again. "All kinds of good stuff. What do you want? How about ribs and crab cakes to start?"

My stomach twisted. I wasn't hungry. But I nodded anyway. It would make Grandma happy for Dad to make a nice dinner for Grandpa coming home.

"Sure enough. That's a great idea, Matty. I'll go out to the store. First I've got to make a list." He rummaged around in Grandma's junk drawer and pulled out a pencil and a pad of paper. Sometimes it caught me off guard how he knew where she kept everything but then I remembered that he grew up in that house too. He still remembered some things.

Maybe we could sit down to a meal and talk things out. I was not going to be hungry but that wasn't the point. If everyone was having a good enough time together maybe they'd realize that breaking us up was a bad idea.

"Let me go to the store with you," I said. I didn't want to be in the house by myself.

"No. I just need to get a few things. The ribs, a couple cans of crabmeat. I'll be back in a little minute."

I wanted to tell him not to spend too much money, but I didn't. I wanted to tell him not to go without me and leave me by myself but I didn't.

I wanted to tell him to come back as soon as he could. But I didn't.

***

Grandma called to say Grandpa needed to stay at the hospital another night. He had a fever. The doctors wanted to keep him to make sure he was okay. She wanted to stay with him because he was getting depressed from being away from home. She did that sometimes when he went to the hospital. They pulled out a cot for her to sleep on so that he didn't have to be alone. It gave the nurses a break so nobody minded.

"You'll be okay for a night, right Matty?" she asked. "Maybe you and your dad can have some time together."

Except that Dad still wasn't home from the grocery store run he left for three and a half hours ago.

I shook out Jester's bag so that the weed settled on the bottom. I packed a couple of sweatshirts over the top of it in case a cop stopped me on the street. I didn't know what covering it with sweatshirts would do for me if that happened but I did it anyway.

To tell the truth I wasn't made for a life of crime.

***

Jester's house was dark. It looked like nobody lived there and nobody was inside. He

264

was sitting on the concrete steps in front. I didn't even see him at first. The ember of his cigarette flared in the grey shadows.

I tossed him the bag. "So where are we going?" I asked.

"Nowhere yet. Got to wait for Alex." Jester was quiet but not relaxed. He took out another cigarette and pressed it to the tip of the one he was smoking. I thought he meant to offer it to me. I got ready to refuse it but he ground out the end of his old cigarette and started smoking the new one himself.

"It's just weed right? I thought you said weed was no big deal," I said. I didn't understand why he was so freaked out.

"This guy owes Alex ten thousand dollars. He's been owing him. That kind of money is always a big deal."

"Who is it?" I had a sick feeling deep in my stomach.

"I don't know. Stop asking questions."

Alex rolled up. There was no music

playing this time. My instinct was to run away as fast as I could. I had to force myself to walk towards that car. Jester got in the front seat and I got in the back. Alex looked straight ahead. He tore away from the curb before Jester even had the door closed.

"You got it?" he asked. The muscles in his jaw jumped. He was wound up even tighter than Jester.

"Yeah." Jester opened a big and the rich smell of weed took over the car. He sealed it back up and rolled down his window.

"We're doing this quick," Alex said. "This asshole owes me. He'll want to see everything is there and that's cool but I'm not standing around. We're getting this over with."

"Okay," Jester said.

"Just don't talk. Don't say anything."

We drove a ways out of town past houses and the mall. He pulled into a gas station and mini mart by the freeway overpass.

We parked by the place where you put

air in your tires. There was another car already there with a man and a lady inside. I could only see the backs of their heads. They didn't look over at us when we pulled up.

"Is that him?" Jester asked.

"Shut up," Alex said. "Get out with the bag."

Jester obeyed without a word. Alex put an arm over the back of the seat. "You," he said. The space between his eyebrows was pinched in angry lines. "Jester says you can drive. Climb over."

I did as he said as he got out. "Be ready to go," he said in a low voice, sticking his head in the window.

My hands were slippery on the steering wheel. The car shook in its own mini earthquake as the engine idled.

My heart raced. A car drove by the gas station, its lights receding down the road in the darkness. Jester and Alex were on the passenger side of the other car. The driver was turned away. I couldn't see him.

Then Jester cussed. His voice broke like back when we were in eighth grade. I laughed even though I was nervous.

Then there were gunshots.

***

My memories are mixed up. The first gunshot was so close it blasted my eardrums and after that every sound was muffled like I was underwater.

Alex slammed his body into the passenger side next to me and screamed at me to go.

"Where's Jester?" I asked. I looked into the backseat as though I expected to see him there. He wasn't.

Alex grabbed the steering wheel and tried to kick my foot off the brake. But we were forgetting Jester. Everything was coming to me really slow.

I got out of the car. Somebody was out there shooting but we couldn't leave without Jester. Alex slid behind the wheel and roared out of the station with the door swinging open.

Another gunshot.

The other backed up so fast it almost ran into a gas pump. The lady in the passenger seat hung her arm out the window, holding a handgun black as oil. I recognized her witchy face. Even through my wasted eardrums I heard the roar of another shot and something hit me hard on the arm. My first thought with that the car hit me but that was impossible. It was driving away from me, not towards me. My ears rang. The lady raised the gun again.

I staggered back. The face of the driver came into the glow of the yellow lights. His face was twisted with panic. His eyes met mine in the second before he yanked the steering wheel and turned the car away.

They bounced down over the curb and sped towards the freeway. The man in the mini mart came running out, yelling I guess. I didn't know what he was saying. I couldn't hear anything anymore.

Jester lay crumpled on the greasy blacktop by the air pumps. His hair fanned out in a puddle of antifreeze. He held his hand over a place high on his chest like he was saying the pledge of allegiance. Blood oozed through his fingers. It ran in lines down his knuckles.

His eyes gazed around. He gagged. I tried to take off my shirt to put over the bloody place on Jester's chest but my right arm wouldn't move. I looked down and my sleeve was soaked in blood. I was confused. Jester's blood could not get all over me so fast. Then I saw that it was my blood. It flowed hot down my arm but I didn't know from where because it didn't hurt.

Sirens wailed in the distance. They were impossibly far away. They would never get to us in time. I pressed down on Jester's hand. Our blood mixed together and ran into the oil on the blacktop. Jester closed his eyes. His blood pulsed and poured in hot gushes no matter how hard I pushed down. It was like his heart beat under my hand, each thump pushing out more.

The sirens were so far away. We would be stuck there forever waiting for help that would never come. I closed my eyes and tried to pray but all I could see was the eyes of the man on the driver's side of the other car. They were the same light brown eyes as mine, inherited from the same woman who loved us both so much that she believed that we were better men than we were turning out to be.

My dad's eyes.

19
A Man of Honor

People ask me what it felt like to be shot. It felt like being hit by a car. Then again, I have never been hit by a car so I don't know for sure. Getting shot didn't even hurt at first. It hurt the next day. It hurt for a lot of days.

On the blacktop Jester was bleeding and bleeding. There was pressure in my ears. The mini mart guy was yelling but I could barely hear him. Spit was flying out of his mouth.

I kept thinking that Jester wasn't going to die. His eyes rolled to the back of his head so just the whites showed. An ambulance.

Police. They pulled me off him. The crowded around so I couldn't see my friend anymore. The backs of people in blue were in my way like a wall.

Then attention on me. A strap tying my arm to my chest.

Jester wasn't going to die. I knew that much. A big neck brace for Jester, a stretcher. His face looking up at the moon. The mini mart guy's spit on my cheek. A cop was asking me something. Hollering because I wouldn't answer. I didn't want to disobey a police officer. I couldn't hear him very well. It was hard to move. I couldn't stop staring at them put Jester in the ambulance.

Then I remember nothing for a while.

***

In my weird half sleep I floated up and heard the constant murmur of Grandma praying. I wanted to talk. I wanted to tell her I was not hurt. Where was Jester? I couldn't talk. I couldn't even open my eyes. I sank back down.

***

When I woke up it seemed that days must have passed by but it was only the next morning. Grandma passed me a drink of water. She fussed around my bed. Keeping busy always calmed her down. A policeman poked his head in and wanted to talk to me right away. I asked Grandma to leave the room.

Snitch. Snitch. The name reeled through my head like bad background music the whole time I answered questions. I snitched on myself, I snitched on Jester. I told the police about Alex, though the funny thing was I never saw Alex with any drugs, guns or money. Jester was right about him being a careful dude. The only thing I knew for sure was that Alex jumped me on the way home from school. I told the police about that too.

I answered questions but I didn't ask any. I was afraid to ask about Jester. No one was telling me anything. My fingernails were caked with his blood. I still felt it flowing between our fingers, gushing with every beat of his heart. Jester was the livingest person I had ever known. He couldn't stop moving. He couldn't stop breathing.

The policemen wanted to know more information than I had about the meet up. Jester hadn't told me anything about the deal. There were a lot of questions I couldn't answer. The cop taking notes clicked his pen open and closed a million times. He was getting frustrated and I didn't blame him.

"Did you know the woman with the gun?" the policeman asked.

"Ask the guy who was driving," I said.

"Who was he?"

"My father," I said.

The cop raised his eyebrows. Maybe he thought it was a joke.

My room must have been on the same side of the building as Mr. Manlow. The freeway ran beneath the window like a vein. I looked out the window. The conversation with the cop was making me tired. Outside, cars bunched up and then moved along in rush hour traffic like a long shiny inchworm. No matter what, people still went to work. They still drove home at the end of the day. The world didn't stop for anybody.

"Your father?" the policeman said.

"Daniel Sullivan," I said. "My *dad*." Whatever that word meant.

The policeman made me tell the same story four times. My arm ached and the pain was growing, but I just grit my teeth. I wanted to feel it. He clicked his pen closed after the fourth time through the questions. My throat was dry.

"You're lucky to be alive," he said.

I exhaled. I hadn't known that I had been holding my breath. He patted me on the shoulder of the arm that was bandaged. Pain shot through the arm and up the side of my neck. I made a face but he acted like he didn't notice. The cop talked to me about learning my lesson and about staying away from drugs and people who sold them.

"Whatever game you are in, young man, get out. I see too many dead kids in my job. Listen to what I am telling you," he said. His voice was shaky. "Your friend last night, he was just one dead boy of too many," he said.

I looked up at the ceiling and let tears run down my face and in rivers into the pillow under my head.

20
A Strong Core

I went home in three days. Grandma treated me like I had the flu instead of a bullet hole through my arm. She kept bringing me chicken soup and ginger ale. I didn't mind, to tell the truth. It was nice to be treated like a kid, if only for a while.

The day before Jester's funeral I sat in my room looking up whatever I could find about what happened that night. The police picked up my dad. There was a short police log about it on the local news online. I tried to imagine the scene. It didn't say if he fought them or if he just gave up. He didn't try very hard to get away. They found him and his girlfriend or whatever at a motel in the mountains not even fifty miles from town. Their big plan must have been to steal Jester's weed and run off with the drugs *and* the money.

Grandma brought up a tray with soup, crackers and more ginger ale. She set it down on my desk without saying anything. She kept her eyes away from the computer screen. She raked her fingers into my hair, twisting it into pieces. She didn't say anything about how I needed a barber. She just clutched me around the ears with both hands and hugged my whole head.

"Okay, Grandma," I said. I had to let her do all that baby stuff to me. She'd been through enough.

She patted my cheek and left without saying anything. We didn't talk much when I was in the hospital. She was being so quiet since I got home that if she wasn't so kissy

and huggy all the time I would have thought
that she was mad at me. I waited until she
closed the door and went back to searching
the name *Daniel Sullivan*.

After a couple days there was a longer
story about it that said my dad claimed he
didn't have anything to do with it. His story
was full of lies. It wasn't his plan. He was just
the driver. He barely knew the woman with the
gun. He'd just met her at a bar that day. Right
away I knew that wasn't true because he had
her overnight at our house the night before. As
far as I knew he was lying about everything.
The lady said he was lying. She was trying to
say that she was my dad's girlfriend. The truth
was probably somewhere in the middle of the
pile of lies.

At least now I knew what Dad was
using Grandma's money for. He wanted it for
his little business deals. Her money was gone
forever now. My grandparents and I were
caught in a spider web created by the lies and

crimes of my dad and me. I had court dates coming up and Mrs. Grimes was my lawyer. All of the things my dad and I did wrong were crossed and connected. My grandmother was caught in it. She went around the house looking after Grandpa and me like usual but she was so quiet now. I caught her shaking her head every now and then like she was confused.

I watched her sadness knowing that I was part of what created it. I had tried to help. I had made everything worse.

***

Reverend Foster and the church ladies made a memorial for Jester. His dad wasn't there. I guess Jester had an aunt and a few cousins in Nevada. Nobody from his family answered any of Mrs. Foster's calls. His father didn't want to have anything to do with us. He wouldn't tell us if he was burying Jester or cremating him or what.

I sat in the front pew next to Grandpa. He held my hand. I didn't know whether or not he understood fully what was going on but he made me feel better.

Mike and his parents sat towards the back. The Grimes family was there too, but they didn't ask me to sit with them. Coach and Jessica were giving me the silent treatment. Mrs. Grimes told me at the end of one of our meetings about my court dates that I needed to give them time. She said that forgiving me would take time but that they would come around to it if only I could be patient. I felt their eyes on the back of my head but I didn't turn around. I was too ashamed. I hoped Mrs. Grimes was right about them forgiving me because I would never forgive myself.

Grandma had invited me to make a speech or whatever about Jester at the memorial but I didn't want to. She didn't force me. I didn't know what to say except that I was sorry that my dad's girlfriend shot him dead. I was sorry my dad just drove off and left my friend and me to die. But more than that, I was sorry for not talking Jester out of going to the meet up in the first place. I was sorry that I never once tried to talk him out of selling weed. Instead of being his friend I offered to be his business partner and then smoked with him without even paying for my share. When I thought about it too much my own guilt in Jester's death was so plain to me that I didn't know why the cops didn't just arrest me and stick me in jail forever.

The choir sang a couple of songs. Mrs. Grant went up and talked about how good Jester was in math. He took Geometry in ninth grade and she was on him to take the Honors Algebra and Trigonometry class in sophomore year. I didn't know she wanted him in Honors. It was hard to imagine. Jester never talked about it. Then again, I'd never asked him.

Then Grandma went up. She didn't use

the microphone. Her voice was plenty loud without it.

"Jesse was my grandson's friend, but I didn't do anything for him. Tell the truth in the past six months I hardly saw him. I knew he could have used a meal or two with family. I knew he could have used someone to look after him.

"You all gave me an honor when my roof came down. You clapped your hands for me and gave me a nice fern and I accepted it with pride in my heart. But you should know that Jesse came to my house just last month and I might as well have kicked him off my porch. I did not invite him in. I thought, that boy is trouble. I thought, I hope he does not get my Matty in trouble. But I never once thought of lending out my hand to ease *his* trouble. I thought you should know that." She clamped her mouth shut then. She sat down so hard the bench shook.

I pressed my hands down flat on the

cool smooth wood of the pew. Of all the people who should have been blaming themselves, it should not have been my grandmother. It should have been me. I pressed down on the pew until my hurt arm twanged and throbbed and made me remember.

The choir sang a song about how if you have a friend in this world, then God has been doubly good to you. It was okay but I hoped it was the last song. I wanted to go home.

***

Based on the work I did and my test scores, Mrs. Grant passed me in summer school Algebra with an A even though I missed the last couple of days and the final. She put a note in with my report card that said she hoped to see me in Honors Geometry instead of the regular Geometry. I thought of Jester being ready for Trig already. He was taking

Honors Geometry while I was pissing away in regular Algebra not even doing my homework.

I didn't know if I was kicked off the football team or what. The physical therapy guy said I could train with the team on lower body stuff but that playing was out for the season at least. Maybe for life. I'd never be as strong in my right arm as I was before getting shot.

Coach Grimes still didn't call or come around in the few days after Jester's memorial. Neither did Jessica. Cassie didn't call. Mike's mother would probably never allow him to even think about me ever again.

Grandma, Grandpa and I hung around the house. The new couch on the new porch sat unused. We stayed inside and watched golf. We watched the game shows. We stayed away from the talk shows.

Even Grandpa was quieter than usual. Grandma and I sat on either side of him in front of the television, each holding one of his hands. We held on to him like we were afraid he might float off away from us again and we needed to hold him down to make him stay.

I skimmed the leaves off of Mr. Manlow's pool and I watered his flowers. I reread the chapter on *Manly Body*. I did sit-ups in my room. *You must build up your core muscles. You must have inside strength in order to be a Manly man.*

I did push-ups with my good arm. I thought about my core. I prayed for inside strength.

21
Jessica

I rode my bike to where the Grimes family lived because Mrs. Grimes wanted me to come over and talk about what I should wear and what I should say to the judge in a couple of days.

She met me at the door and told me to leave my bike in the garage. We sat in the office in their house and talked things over. I liked talking to Mrs. Grimes. Whenever we got together I felt that these problems would not be what my life was about forever. I wouldn't always hear gunshots in my head. I wouldn't always close my eyes at night and see my dad's face through the windshield of that car, seeing right through me.

Mrs. Grimes talked a lot about "getting this behind us." The air conditioning in their house dried the sweat off my skin. I always wanted to stand up straighter when I was there.

I sat in a leather chair across from her desk. She put on her reading glasses and looked over some papers from the District Attorney. She looked like Jessica when she did that.

"Well, I have some good news," she said. "You aren't facing charges. You won't have to go to court."

"But I told the police everything," I said.

"It's good you told the truth to the police," she said. "The charges of possession with intent to sell are being dropped. It doesn't surprise me, Matthew. Whatever happened before, you weren't in possession of anything that night. The only reason you were there was to protect Jester."

"Don't say that," I said. "It's because of me that he's dead."

Mrs. Grimes gave me a strange look. "Do you believe that?"

"Think about it," I said. "You know it's true." I felt like I was choking so I stopped talking. Part of me wasn't relieved that I wasn't going to be facing charges. I deserved to have something happen to me after what happened to Jester.

"You're wrong," she said. "It isn't your fault."

I just shrugged. I wasn't going to argue with Mrs. Grimes. She was a lawyer and she would win an argument. That didn't change what I knew was true.

We were almost done when Coach Grimes and Jessica came home. Coach stuck his head in and nodded at his wife.

"Come in," she said.

Coach looked like he didn't want to. He held on to the doorjamb with one hand. "I've got things to do," he said. "I'll stay out of your hair."

"Come in," she said again. Her voice was hard. She didn't look like Jessica anymore. Now she reminded me of Grandma. Coach sighed and took one step in.

I looked down at my hands on my lap. The veins in my forearms popped out. I hoped he noticed. I wanted to tell him about how many push ups I was doing a day now but I knew it would be stupid. I knew it wouldn't make up for anything.

"I'm sorry, Coach," I blurted. "I let you down."

"You let yourself down," he said. "I don't think I know who you are."

I bit the inside of my cheek to keep from crying. "Kyle," Mrs. Grimes said. She sounded disappointed in both of us.

"I'm sorry too," Coach said. "I'm not

ready to speak to him yet, Nia." He left the room. I could hear him talking to Jessica in another part of the house.

"He'll come around." Mrs. Grimes didn't smile but she winked. She hugged me on my way out. It was awkward but nice too. When she hugged me I could tell she was strong, like *her* core could hold up her family and everybody else she knew who needed it.

I walked my bike out of the garage. The sun was setting and the day's heat radiated off the ground. I wanted to give Jessica time to come out and talk to me if she wanted to so I crouched down in the driveway and pretended to work on my bike chain.

"What are you doing?" Jessica marched out. Her fists rested on her hips. She wore shorts and an Alhambra Dragons t-shirt. The muscles in her legs were crazy. As mad as she was at me I couldn't help noticing.

"What are you looking at?" she said.

"Sorry," I said. "I'm just fixing my bike."

"Nothing's wrong with your bike."

"I know. I wanted to talk to you and I needed an excuse."

She shook her head. "That's just the way you do, Matty. You don't tell the truth. You make an excuse. You're too much of a knucklehead just to come up to somebody and say you want to talk."

"I want to talk."

"So talk."

My tongue was fat in my mouth.

"I'm sorry." I said.

"For what?" She didn't get even a little bit soft. Nowhere in her eyes was my friend who brought me barbeque or kept me from smashing Grandma's Santa.

"I'm sorry for getting shot," I said.

She sighed and moved her weight to one hip like I had given the wrong answer to a very simple question.

"That wasn't your fault," she said. "You think I hate you because somebody shot you?"

293

"You hate me?" I asked.

"What? No." Her eyes shifted and got shiny like they were wet. "God, Matthew. I was so scared when I heard. You could have been killed."

I thought of my dad's girlfriend's face, her mean eyes. She *would* have killed me if she got a better shot. I had no doubt of that.

"I'm sorry anyway," I said. I didn't know what else to say. "You're so mad at me. I screwed up. I know that." If I couldn't stop crying at everything nobody was going to take me seriously. I wiped my eyes with the back of my hand.

"You didn't trust me," Jessica said. Her voice caught in the back of her throat and it seemed like she was going to cry too. "I told you that you had friends. You could have come to me. My mom and dad were already talking about ways to help you and your grandparents out. But you couldn't wait for that. You had to go off and do things your way."

She hit herself on the top of her head as if the sheer volume of my stupidity was too much to handle. "You always said you were alone. But every time you needed somebody, I was there. I was always there and you didn't even see me."

She had me. I couldn't think of a single thing to say to that. She was right. Jessica was always there for me. Even at the beginning of the summer when she caught me with my Grandma at the Hefty Boys, Jessica had my back. She didn't tell anybody about finding me under that big sign with the happy smiley fat kid on it. She never even made fun of me for it when nobody was around. She could have too. I wouldn't have blamed her. I probably would have laughed right along with her. But she never laughed at me, not once.

"Why?" I asked.

"Why what?" She shielded her eyes against the low evening sun.

"Why were you so nice to me?"

"You don't know why?"

I shrugged and felt dumber than I ever had before in my entire life. She threw her arms out and I thought she might either hit me or hug me. I was hoping for a hug. Instead, she marched back towards her house. At the door, she turned around and then strode back towards me where I still stood by my bike like a dummy.

"Because I *like* you, Matt. I really like you. I *like* like you. Do you understand now?"

"I like you too," I said. And it was true. It was true before I even realized it. I liked Jessica so much. I just wanted to be around her. She made me feel comfortable and good about myself most of the time. I didn't feel too great when she was yelling at me. But I would rather she yell at me than ignore me.

"I really like you, Jessica. I *like* you like you."

Her forehead unknotted for a tiny

second. She tilted her head. I thought of the clovers tickling my feet on the lawn the day I helped rebuild the porch. I wanted to go back in time to that day.

"Well I'm still mad," Jessica said. She stamped her foot, but then she touched the toe of my shoe with her shoe. Like maybe she wasn't that mad.

"Okay," I said.

"I'll talk to you tomorrow."

"Okay," I said again.

She went back to her house for real this time. I was sorry to see her go but she looked really nice walking away.

I got on my bike and rode home. I didn't one hundred percent understand what had just happened between Jessica Grimes and me. It didn't make logical sense for me to be smiling. My friend was dead. My dad was in prison and my arm was still killing me from being shot through by his girlfriend.

I stood up on the pedals and rode as fast

as I could. The wind blew on my face and roared in my ears. It didn't make sense. But I was smiling.

22
Tad Manly

The day before Mr. Manlow was due home from the hospital, I decided to unpack his boxes. When he came home he would find his shelves filled with books and football statues. Not only that, I would clean his house. That way he could get strong again in a fresh clean place.

I had big ideas but I did not know how difficult this would be with only one good arm. My gunshot arm was getting better but it didn't move so great. The physical therapy I had to do to make it stronger made football workouts seem like a gentle frolic in a meadow. It was a whole new level of pain.

After a few hours of vacuuming and dusting and putting away Mr. Manlow's five million books, I wished I had someone to help me. I never knew a man with so many books. He had books on everything. He had Greek myths and four different Bibles and books about history and art and sports. There was no way he could have read all of those books unless he read every single day of his life.

I thought of calling Jessica but I was afraid to after she yelled at me and then said she liked me. So far I wasn't that great with girls. Jessica had said she liked me. She said she *liked* liked me, and until we had another chance to get together for her to say different, that fact still stood as true. Jessica Grimes liked me. That was the best thing about my life. Every time I thought about her I got a feeling like Christmas and a roller coaster. I wasn't going to mess it up by asking her to come over and help me clean an old man's dirty house.

The only problem was that Jessica would have hated it if she knew I needed help and didn't call. I lifted books with one hand and had an imaginary argument with her in my head. *You're not alone*, Jessica would say. It would make her madder to see me there sweating it out with one good arm than it would for me to call her up. But I guess I was like my Grandma that way. I didn't like to ask for help.

I took a break and got a glass of water. I stood in the cool air in front of the open refrigerator and tugged up the waistband of my shorts. The elastic was all worn out. My shorts were annoying because they felt like they were about to fall down any second. I needed new clothes. I took a sip of water. What I really wanted was an ice cold Coke, but I always chose water now.

Water is the best drink. Water is the drink of champions. Tad Manly. The person I used to be, the one who looked for answers in an old book stolen from a yard sale, seemed like a kid to me now. I wasn't ashamed of it exactly, but I still didn't let anyone know I read a self-help book. I kept it stashed between my mattress and box spring like it was something dirty. I had thought *How to Be Manly* would help me get everything I wanted. I would be able to turn into a different guy by the end of a summer just by getting cut muscles. I had thought that the meaning of my life would be complete if Cassie Bale would only be my girlfriend.

Since the shooting, Cassie had never called me once. Not even to ask if I was okay.

I set down the glass and picked up a pair of scissors. The smell of the roses in the backyard blew in on a breeze through the open windows. Cleaned up and cleared of boxes, it wasn't a bad house. It was like ours except that Mr. Manlow had a bunch of football stuff instead of Grandma's Santa statues and cake plates. I left the boxes marked *Thaddeus* for last. I had no idea what was in them or where I would put whatever it was. There wasn't any more shelf space. I cut the tape sealing the box. When I opened the flaps, yet another book rested on the top.

The book was a copy of *How to Be Manly* by Tad Manly. It was like seeing a ghost. I opened it and there was a note on the inside cover.

To Dad: You taught me everything. I hope you like the book. Love, Thaddeus.

Underneath the book were pictures, plaques, trophies, newspaper clippings, and all of the things Mr. Manlow always wanted to show me about his son's football career. I had always thought that he meant to talk about his son's high school football career, but there were photos of a college team, then stories about NFL picks. I leafed through it and then looked closely at the high school varsity team picture. The uniforms were nearly the same as ours and the players could have been my teammates except for their goofy hairdos.

Then I looked again through the names.

Thaddeus Stanley Manlow. Front row, center. I stared at the guy smiling at the camera on one knee. I knew that guy.

It was Tad Manly.

I sat down on the floor hard. Tad Manly was Bob Manlow's son.

I ended up calling Jessica for help after all.

***

Jessica got on one side of Mr. Manlow and I supported him on the other. He didn't want to use a walker when he went through his own front door at last. His arm felt like a bird's wing.

The nurse who was going to be looking after him at night had already been in the house making sure all the handrails were put in and non-slip stuff placed on the floors. He wasn't going to have to go into a nursing home because he was going to have nurses come to his house.

"Slow down, Matthew," he said. "I'm not ready to go for a run yet."

I apologized. I was excited to get inside.

Grandma held Grandpa's hand and followed behind. Grandpa's face was healed from his fall but he looked weaker to me since he came home. Grandma said he didn't remember his hours wandering alone by the canal, but I wondered. He seemed more confused and distant since we got him back. He smiled about visiting Mr. Manlow's house, though. I was glad to see him happy.

We brought Mr. Manlow into his living room, where Jessica and I had a surprise waiting. Mr. Manlow didn't notice it at first. He sat down in his big chair and looked around. "Why are you all standing around like that?" he asked. "You're making me feel like I just came back from the dead."

I was shy all of a sudden. Jessica punched me lightly on my good shoulder, but I was frozen. She went to go stand by the big trophy case she and her dad had carried into the house that morning.

"Oh my," Mr. Manlow said.

He tried to stand on his own as if he forgot about his broken hip. Jessica dashed forward and together we helped him up.

"What did you do?" he whispered.

In the glass case were all of Tad Manly's high school awards and trophies, his college bowl awards, newspaper clippings about being the first NFL draft pick. We even put in school photos from when he was the fat smiling kid I knew so well from the book.

There was a long article about him in *Sports Illustrated*. It told the story of how Thaddeus Manlow became known as Tad Manly by his sophomore year of college. He had a way of taking care of business on and off the field that made fans and commentators call him Manly. He was an enormous and threatening wall of pain charging down the field so commentators thought it was ironic to call him Tad. Besides, Tad was a nickname for Thaddeus and so it stuck. He was known for being a good guy. Several of his teammates called him their "brother."

We put the articles about the car accident that took his life in the lower right hand corner. There was a yellowed newspaper photo of the crumpled car, the story of the drunk driver that had killed them both while Tad Manly was at the top of his career. He'd just written a book, the article said. He'd dedicated it to his father.

Jessica wanted to leave the stuff about his death out of the case, but I voted to leave it in. Tad Manly's death was part of the story too. Mr. Manlow was not the kind of man who would want to deny the truth even if it hurt.

It was quiet while Mr. Manlow gazed at

the case. Grandma held her fingers to her lips and Grandpa smiled as though he was listening to music no one else could hear. Jessica stood beside Mr. Manlow. She helped him move from left to right to take it all in. He paused in front of the picture of the totaled car. *Tad Manly Killed*. I was afraid to look at Mr. Manlow. I hoped I was right to put that in. I just kept my own eyes on the article and forced myself to read the headline again. I wasn't even born yet when he died. It had happened in an instant and then this great man, Mr. Manlow's son, was dead. The drunk driver who killed him didn't survive the wreck either. There wasn't anyone left to be mad at. There wasn't anyone left behind to love or hate.

"I miss him," Mr. Manlow said, his voice deep and sure. He didn't sound as old as he looked. "Do you know that? After almost twenty years of him being gone. I wake up every morning and I miss my son."

Mr. Manlow moved his hand to tell us to bring him back to his chair. He groaned as we lowered him down. I had so many questions. I had so many things I wanted to say.

"Who is responsible for this?" Mr. Manlow asked. I couldn't tell if he was mad or happy.

I cleared my throat. "It was my idea," I said. "I thought it would be nice to come home to and everything. We can take it out if you want. I probably should have asked first."

"Nonsense," he said. Then he took my hand and pulled me down so that our faces were close together.

"Thank you," he said. I avoided his eyes but his grip tightened. He pulled me down closer. I took a deep breath and lifted my eyes to look into his. I didn't want to. I was still ashamed.

But the look on his face made my shame go away. It felt like he was looking deep into my thoughts, into my heart. He was seeing me and it was uncomfortable and peaceful at the same time. He nodded just a tiny nod so that only I could see it. I saw what Tad Manly was talking about now when he talked about his father. He was lucky to have a dad like that.

"Thank you," he repeated.

I shook his hand, making sure to have a strong grip. "You're welcome," was all I said.

23

Here Comes Santa Claus

The day after we moved Mr. Manlow back into his house, Coach Grimes came over. He asked Grandma if he and I could talk on the porch by ourselves. Grandma brought us lemonades and let us be.

I thought he was there to tell me he was officially kicking me off the football team. Even if my arm did work right, Coach couldn't have a guy on the team who went to a drug deal. He gave us so many lectures against drugs that he would look like a punk if he backed down on his own rule. If you got in any trouble with drugs you were off the team, no questions asked.

But it was sad anyway. I felt like one of those soldiers in old movies who get in trouble so the captain or whoever rips the stripes off his shirt. I knew I deserved it but it was still embarrassing. I invited Coach to sit down on the couch with me so we could get it over with.

Coach Grimes took a long sip of lemonade. Then he cleared his throat. Then he took another drink. The lawn sprinklers came on.

"Damn," I said out loud by mistake.

"Excuse me?"

"No, sorry Coach. It's just the sprinklers. I fixed them yesterday but I got the timer wrong. They were supposed to come on in the morning."

"Oh," he said. He seemed nervous. I wished he would just start yelling at me like Jessica did. Clear the air. "So you fixed your grandmother's sprinkler yesterday?"

"I had to fix the system. Install a new timer. Mr. Parker from church has been showing me how to do stuff around the house. Grandma hasn't been talking about selling since everything happened, so I'm hoping if I keep on top of it she'll keep it and let me stay."

"You were real busy yesterday, weren't you?"

"Sir?" I wondered when the yelling was going to start. Maybe he'd make me do push-ups on the lawn with the sprinklers going. It would be a whole lot less awkward than sitting on the couch trying to understand what Coach wanted to talk about.

"Yesterday you and Jessica were busy fixing up the trophy case for your neighbor. Tad Manly's father."

"I didn't know Mr. Manlow was Tad Manly's dad until I started unpacking his stuff," I said.

"Tad Manly played for Alhambra his senior year. I was just a kid at the time. Used to go to the games. When I played in high school we all looked up to him. Tad Manly was living the dream, you know?"

I nodded. Tried to be still. Coach's voice was quieter than I ever heard him talk. He made me nervous as hell when he was being nice. He looked off across the lawn like he was going down memory lane in his head.

"Then he was killed right at the peak of his career. Before the peak, even. Jessica said he wrote a book."

"Yeah. *How to Be Manly* it's called." I waited for him to make fun of it but he didn't.

"Huh. I should read that sometime. See if I can get a copy."

I was about to tell him I had a copy up in my room but I stopped myself. "So why are you here, Coach?" I couldn't stand it anymore. "I thought you weren't talking to me. I already assumed I was off the team."

He looked at me like I was speaking another language. "You're not off the team,

Matthew. I'll have to talk to your doctor about what you can do with that arm, but you're welcome back anytime. As soon as your doctor gives the okay."

"But I thought—"

"Forget what you thought. Listen to me, young man." He started warming up. "I came here to tell you that what happened to Jester is not your fault. Mrs. Grimes told me you blame yourself. She says that you think you deserve to go to jail because your friend is dead. Well, you deserve a lot of things, but you do not deserve jail. I'll tell you that right now."

"Okay," I said.

"And let me tell you something else. With all due respect to your grandmother, I thought she was dead wrong at the memorial service the other day. I could barely sit and listen to her blaming herself for that boy's death, wondering why she didn't ask him over more. Jester had the same choices and opportunities as everybody else. He could have gone out for a sport. He already had Mrs. Grant reaching out to him. If your grandmother felt she needed to protect you from a bad influence then that is what she had to do. Jester made choices in life. What happened was a tragedy and I'm real sad it happened. But it was not the fault of the good people he was pushing away while he did what he did. I refuse to accept it."

"Okay."

"If I thought the way your grandmother thinks, I'd lose my mind. Do you know how many kids I've lost since I started coaching and teaching at the high school? I've been doing this ten years. I've lost plenty. If I blamed myself every time a kid got himself thrown in jail or killed I'd have to quit my job."

I nodded and I really did understand what he was saying. I didn't think I agreed with him, but I got his argument.

"That was why I was so angry with you. I could tell you were in trouble and I made

316

myself available to help. But you didn't take it."

"I'm sorry, Coach. I thought I could handle everything on my own. Everything with my dad was a mess and I thought I could clean it up by myself."

He put his arm around me and he pulled me close in a sort of side hug. He shook me so my teeth rattled together.

"We're not meant to do everything alone. That's why we have friends. We're like a big team backing you up, son, but you have to back us up too. By not doing stupid shit."

"I know," I said. It was weird to hear him cuss. I didn't think I ever heard him cuss before.

"That was a great thing you did for that old man," he said.

"Thanks for letting us have the trophy case, " I said. "It looks great. You should come over and see it later."

"I will, I will," he said. "But it was you and Jessica that had the idea and did all the work.

Not a lot of kids would think to do something like that for a neighbor. I was real proud when I heard about it. Of both of you."

"Thanks."

"You see, when Jessica told me about you welcoming Mr. Manlow home by honoring his son, I knew that you really were the young man I always thought. You made a few mistakes—"

"I learned from my mistakes, Coach. I really did."

He smiled. "I know." He patted my back. "You better have or you'll be sorry."

He flexed his biceps and raised his hands over his head. He was threatening to lift me like a barbell, just like the rumor of what he did with George. I scooted to the other side of the couch. I really did not want him to lift me. "You couldn't do it, Coach. I am too heavy, even for you."

"Don't be so sure, son." Coach stood up. "You're pretty lean these days. I could lift you one-handed if I wanted to." He winked and went inside to talk to Grandma.

I paused for a second and then ran up to my room. I grabbed something and then ran back down to catch him before he left.

"Here," I said. I pushed the book into Coach Grimes' hand. "I should have given it to Jester. Maybe you know some other kid who might need it."

Coach flipped through the pages.

"Maybe I'll read it myself," he said. "I could learn a thing or two from Tad Manly."

"You already know all of it," I said. "You're great." My face got hot. I sounded like a dummy. At one time or another I'd given the entire Grimes family had reason to think I must have lost my mind.

But Grimes acted like what I said was okay. "I love you too, son," he said. Then he hugged me so hard my arm hurt but I didn't care.

***

Two weeks passed and Grandma still wouldn't talk to me about the money. She wouldn't talk to me about my dad. I returned to weight training with the team but I wasn't going to be able to run plays. If I got hit in the arm the wrong way I could mess it up. The doctors said that they weren't sure whether or not there would be permanent ligament damage. Playing for the season was out of the question. They didn't know yet about next year.

So I went to practices and ran stairs or trained in the weight room while the rest of the guys got ready for the season. I could hear them while I did leg presses and I tried not to get jealous. After so many workouts when I cursed the grass on that field and wanted to go home, I never thought I would feel so bad for not getting to run across it with the rest of the team.

One day at the very end of the summer I did fix-ups around the house after practice. I got out this how-to book for basic home repairs that Mr. Parker gave me. I replaced a rubber washer in the kitchen faucet. Sometimes Mr. Parker came over after dinner and showed me how to do different stuff like replace the sealing on the refrigerator door so that it closed like it was supposed to. He said I learned fast. It was fun for me. I was getting good at fixing things. I enjoyed it. When I could fix something that was broken, I got the satisfaction of making something right. Even a little thing like the faucet working made our lives easier and I was the one who made it happen.

In the garage, I found a yellow sticker on one of Grandpa's wrenches. My first day back from the hospital I went around one-handed and picked off every last one of the yellow yard sale stickers my dad put on everything. Every now and then I would find one I missed.

Whenever I did I peeled it off and flicked it into the garbage. I also threw his things from the guest room into a big black trash bag and flung it into a spidery corner of the garage and considered it a big step towards never having to think of him again.

Someday soon I would throw the bag into the garbage.

That's what I told myself. But when I wasn't paying attention bad feelings about my dad snuck up on me. I hated to admit it but part of me felt bad that he was stuck in jail. Part of me felt guilty about it. Part of me wondered if I had been more interesting or smarter maybe none of this would have happened.

Most of the time I got it that nothing could have changed what happened. The only thing I could do was get rid of the stickers where I found them hiding. With each one gone I took back something that didn't belong to anyone else to sell.

Grandma didn't seem to notice the stickers. When I brought up the matter of paying the bills, she gave me the stink eye and told me to quit asking about it. I was afraid that maybe she was in some kind of shock after everything that happened. She was going about buying groceries and fixing cakes for people and I had no idea what she was using for money.

So I told Mrs. Grimes about it. She listened and wrote down the things I said in a notebook. We came up with a plan. It would make Grandma mad but the only people I knew stronger than Grandma were the Grimes family.

I replaced Grandpa's wrench to its place on the workbench. I kept it as nice and neat as Grandpa did when I was a kid. I looked at the time. It was almost dinner. I needed to take a shower so I could smell nice. Grandma didn't know it, but we were having company.

"Matty, settle down," Grandma said. We were having spaghetti. I had helped make dinner and cooked the entire package of noodles instead of just half. I let Grandma think it was a mistake. I kept looking at the time and I couldn't sit still.

Finally the doorbell rang and I jumped up to get it. Coach Grimes led the way in, and they brought homemade cornbread and acted like Grandma had invited them all along.

I set out plates and napkins and silverware while Mrs. Grimes, Coach and Jessica sat around our table. Grandpa frowned and looked confused. I had hoped that the change in routine wouldn't upset him but he banged on his plate with a spoon.

"Matty, I didn't know we were having guests," Grandma said. She hugged Grandpa from the back, holding down his hand and taking away the spoon.

"We need to talk," I said. "You won't talk to me about money or my dad or anything. I know we're in trouble."

"You don't know anything," Grandma said.

"So I asked for help," I said.

"He did the right thing, Mrs. Sullivan," Coach Grimes said. He tucked a napkin into his shirt. "Boy, this spaghetti sure looks good."

Grandma was not being charmed. "I'm pleased to have you at my table," she said. "You all are always welcome here. But I'm not talking about my private business. Now there is no need to worry. I appreciate your concern, but there is no need." She sat down in her own place and handed Jessica the salad bowl. Jessica looked at me with her eyebrows raised.

"Matthew told us about how much your son took from your accounts," Mrs. Grimes said. Grandma's mouth was in its line. I didn't know how she could remain icy with Mrs.

Grimes. She was so smiling and pretty and talked so soft she could make the devil sorry.

"He should not have done that," Grandma said. "He knows better."

Grandpa sensed that people were unhappy and nervous. He started talking to himself, saying prayers under his breath. I moved my chair to be close to him. When I put my arm around his shoulders he calmed down.

"Mrs. Sullivan, I am surprised at you," said Mrs. Grimes. "I've never known you to act without sense. Let us help you. Let me look over your accounts and see what we can do to help. You're not by yourself in this. You have friends in our family and in the church. We'll all help you get along."

"Don't need help. Thank you kindly."

"What are you going to do?" It was interesting yet horrifying to see Mrs. Grimes get flustered. She flung her hands around when she talked. "Are you going to buy groceries and pay bills on credit until you land yourself out on the street? What will become of your grandson?"

Grandma slammed her hands down on the table. All of the plates and silverware jumped. Coach Grimes looked at his hands in his lap and for once I got a quick look into what he must have been like as a kid.

Without another word, Grandma left the table. But she did not go to her room. She flung open the door into the garage and let it slam against the wall. We could hear her rummaging around in there.

Mrs. Grimes touched my arm. "This kind of thing can happen with old people," she whispered. "It's very difficult for her to come to terms with the fact that she can't do it on her own anymore, do you understand? She's used to being independent."

She smoothed her hair and tugged the ends of her blouse to straighten it. Coach Grimes went into the garage after Grandma.

She barked orders at him and he said, "Yes ma'am." There was the sound of ceramics knocking together.

"Here comes Santa Claus," Grandpa sang.

Jessica laughed. It broke the tension just a little.

Grandpa was right anyhow because Grandma and Coach came back in, Coach carrying an entire box full of Grandma's yard sale Santa Claus statues. She carried an armful herself, their faces peeking out from between her arms. She put each one she was holding down on the tabletop, hard.

I thought she had gone crazy. Jessica watched, her eyes wide. I had never seen Jessica Grimes frightened of anything before. Coach and Mrs. Grimes just looked worried. I thought of my dad's terrible offhand comment about Grandma losing her mind too and I had to admit Grandma was making me very nervous.

She left the Santas all in a row on the table and turned her back on us to get something out of a kitchen drawer. She whisked back around with one of those metal hammers with spikes on it that she used to hit meat with before cooking it. She raised the hammer above her head and with a blow too quick for Jessica or anyone else to stop, she smashed the top of Santa's head to bits.

Grandpa started. Grandma was scaring him but she wasn't concerned with that now. Bunches of money bloomed out of Santa's neck like green paper flowers. Twenties, fifties, hundreds. Grandma stepped back with the hammer and wiped her forehead with her sleeve. "I trusted my son and I shouldn't have," she said. "And for that I'm sorry. I wanted to believe that he was ready to be a father to his own boy." She grabbed my chin in one hand. She seemed to grow tall as a tree. "This fine, beautiful, *good* boy. The best boy in the whole world."

Tears popped into my eyes. Everybody was silent except for Grandma. "My son has a darkness in him that I just could never cure," she said. "It was like he couldn't love. The tragedy of his life is that he never could know how lucky he was to have Matthew for a boy. I'm sorry I didn't realize it sooner. Matthew could have been shot dead because of my blindness and for that I will have to answer to my God."

"Grandma! That was my fault, not yours." I found my voice. She gave me the look that I knew meant the discussion was nearly over if it wasn't already.

"We were just worried, Mrs. Sullivan. That's all," Mrs. Grimes said.

"Like I said, I appreciate your concern." Grandma sat down with the hammer still in one hand. "But please don't suggest I can't look after my grandson."

Coach, Mrs. Grimes, Jessica and I stared at the pile of money scattered on the table. Grandma put the hammer down and replaced her napkin on her lap. She twisted spaghetti noodles around her fork as an elegant lady would.

The other Santas rolled their eyes like they were afraid they were going to be next. Coach Grimes pointed at them.

"Are all of these full of—"

"Uh-huh. Got about four dozen more back in the garage besides. Cake money from fifteen years of baking. Started the Santa Saving System the day Matthew was born. Now please pass your wife's cornbread. It looks nice."

Coach did as he was told.

Grandpa excused himself to watch his after dinner game show. He turned it up loud. The host was shouting and bells were ringing.

The sounds of winning.

24
Phat Matt

Grandma never talked about my dad again until the day before school started.

I was back in the Hefty Boys dressing room. The store was having an end of the summer sale and Grandma wasn't missing it. They only gave the senior citizen discount on Thursdays and Sundays. I begged to be able to go as early in the morning as possible so as to avoid any possible crowds. We skipped church this once and left Grandpa at Mr. Manlow's house for the morning. Mr. Manlow and his daytime nurse liked having Grandpa around. It was nice for Grandma and me to be able to do things like go pants shopping without worrying if Grandpa was going to wander away again.

Grandma stood outside the dressing room door while I took down my shorts and got ready to try on clothes. I wore a pair of old cargo shorts I still had from seventh grade. The belt I wore to keep them up with was frayed and the extra holes I cut in it looked bad. It was a hillbilly belt. I was surprised Grandma let me get away with it.

I had some of my own money to spend from working with Mr. Parker the past Saturday on a job he was doing in town. He was building an extension on somebody's house. It was a chance for me to learn more handyman stuff. I didn't expect to get paid but then at the end of the day Mr. Parker gave me a hundred bucks in cash and asked if I would be available on future Saturdays when he needed the extra hand.

I knew I lost weight but I didn't know how much. Even though I wasn't going to get to play that season, Coach wanted me to weigh in at the next practice like everybody else so that he could record my stats.

I tried not to think about it. It was good to just be part of the team. I ran water to players during scrimmages, and cheered for my teammates. I got to wear the jersey on the field.

"Matty? You okay in there? Hurry up," Grandma said.

I had two sizes. I brought in XXL and XL just in the off chance I could fit into my old size. I tried on the XXL pair first and prayed that they would fit.

They didn't. I pulled them up and let go. They fell to my knees.

I tried on the XL. I tugged the waistband away from my stomach. I looked like one of those guys who lost so much weight that they could fit almost another whole person in their old pants.

I yelled for my grandmother. She came running in. I showed her my pants.

"Well well well," she said. "That's amazing, Matty. I guess I didn't notice. My goodness."

"Ma'am?" the attendant said. "You shouldn't be in the boys dressing room, ma'am. This dressing room is for boys only."

I expected Grandma to let him have it, but she just nodded. "Yes, you're right." She turned to go.

"Grandma!" I held the jeans up with both hands. "I need the next size down."

"The next size down is going to be way too big," the store guy said. "You don't belong in Hefty Boys. Why don't you go to the men's department and see what they have there?"

Grandma looked lost. I met her outside the dressing room. It was too bad that Jessica didn't just happen to be there on the day when I was being ejected from the Hefty Boys and straight into the men's department. The end of my hillbilly belt hung out from under my shirt. Grandma looked at me like she'd never seen it before. She blinked at the belt and then looked at me and laughed.

"Oh, Matty," she said. "We've got to get you something decent to wear."

***

On the first day of school I walked down the hall and I felt like that guy in the Christmas movie who walks around invisible in his own life. He is surrounded by people he knows but they can't see him. That's how I felt because I recognized everybody but almost nobody recognized me.

When I passed Cassie in the hall, she saw me but didn't see me. She was even prettier than usual but I didn't say hello. I wasn't still mad about her and Jack but I knew she wasn't someone I could trust as a friend. Besides that, she was boring. I had to admit it. Jessica liked to talk about sports and music and she could skateboard better than any guy. Nothing about Jessica was boring. I found out new things about her every day.

Just as I was walking away Cassie called my name.

"Matty?" I turned around. Her voice was so loud people turned to look at us. "Matty, is that you?"

"Yeah," I shrugged. I didn't want to be rude but I didn't want to stand around either. Honors Geometry was starting in five minutes and I needed to get a seat next to Jessica in case Mrs. Grant was letting us sit where we wanted. That is, in case Mrs. Grant got abducted by aliens over the summer and they transplanted her personality with the personality of a reasonable human being.

"You look different," Cassie said.

"Oh," I said.

We stood there. She shook out her hair. I used to love it when she did that. Now I thought it made her like she had fleas.

I didn't want to be mean. Maybe Cassie and Jack were happy together. Maybe she called him on the phone in the middle of the night like she used to call me. I didn't know. And the funny thing was, I didn't care.

"I'm not so much with Jack anymore," she said. She tilted her head and looked up at me from under her eyelashes. "I've missed you," she said. Then she took her finger and ran it down my chest under the buttons of my shirt. I stepped back.

"Okay," I said. "Well, I have to go." I headed down the hall. I pulled my shirt straight and didn't look back when she called me again.

Jessica waited outside of Mrs. Grant's classroom. George came up behind me and clapped me on the back. "Hey Fatty Matty," he said.

"That's enough, Georgy Porgey," Jessica said. George followed us into the room.

"Naw man, you're not Fatty Matty anymore." He looked at me like he was seeing me for the first time. Like we hadn't spent most of the summer on the same football field suffering together under Coach Grimes. "We have to give you a new name," he said.

"How about Matthew?" Jessica said. "That is his name, you know." She wore her hair in tight new braids and her lips were shiny. I couldn't stop staring at them. Even though she was irritated I still wanted to kiss her. Suddenly I was glad that Mrs. Grant put us in seating charts. I wasn't going to be able to concentrate on math if I sat anywhere near Jessica Grimes.

Mike came in and sat down in an empty desk next to us. He kept his eyes down. I gave him a light shove and then put up a high five right quick to show no hard feelings. He smiled so big it showed all his teeth and he fived me back. Jessica touched my arm. She knew that I missed being friends with Mike. I'd told her about it.

"How about Phat Matt?" George said, butting in between Mike and me. "Phat with a

p. Get it?" Mike shook his head but he had to laugh.

"We get it," Jessica said, a tiny smile playing on her perfect mouth. I leaned forward and kissed her quick before I chickened out.

I thought George was going to explode. He jumped around and hooted and made obnoxious noises. Jessica rolled her eyes but leaned in for another kiss.

"Thank you," I whispered.

"What for?" she asked.

"I'm just remembering to say thank you," I said.

Mrs. Grant started talking then and bossing us around about doing homework and getting serious since this was an Honors class. To be honest I wasn't even listening at first. I was getting full of something that made me want to laugh and cry at the same time. Right then I said a silent thanks to Tad Manly, to Grandma and Grandpa, to Coach and Mrs. Grimes, to God, to everybody. In that little minute I couldn't say thank you enough.

I wasn't even in nature or in church or anything. I was just in plain old school. Math class. It didn't matter. I wrote my name in my notebook for something to do, but what I felt like doing was singing right out loud. For the first time since the night of the shooting I felt truly and purely okay.

"You're smiling like a goofy person," Jessica said in a whisper. She had no idea how goofy I felt. I just kept smiling until Jessica couldn't help laughing. Mrs. Grant looked over from across the room and told us both to be quiet. Which wasn't fair because she'd started class even though the bell hadn't rung yet. But I didn't care. Gratitude bubbled in me like I was a soda somebody shook up on a warm day.

The bell rang and class started for real. I was going to pay attention this year. I was going for a strong mind, strong body, strong friends. I was going for it all. But I had a matter of strong spirit to take care of first.

Thank you, I said silently to whoever was listening. Thank you for everything.

Acknowledgements

My thanks go to the coaches.

My coaches in publication Rachel Miller and Anna McCormally of Giant Squid Books are literary renegade goddesses of publishing. It has been a true honor to be included in their vision.

My students are my coaches of story. I cheer their heroic journeys from the sidelines with gratitude and hope.

My writing coaches Tricia Ireland Stirling and Vanessa Diffenbaugh believed in this story from the beginning, and helped me tell it in the best way possible. Thank you also to Tod Lippy of Esopus magazine whose attention to art, integrity and stories continue to motivate and inspire.

Laura Alvarez, Evan Hartzell, and Andrew Kjera are my art coaches, and never let me forget what I'm really supposed to be doing and what human beings are for.

Thank you to Lora Schoen, my friendship coach whose belief and magic inspire me to write my stories with courage.

The Squaw Valley Community Writers coached me on dedication to craft. Thank you to all teachers and participants.

Izaiah Skelton, Tre'von Lyle and Genesis Scales were my football coaches. Thanks for answering my nine million questions.

Zeus was my dog coach, the inspiration for Dirty Harry, who taught me how to be a good pet owner, and whose unconditional love I always tried to be worth.

Jim, Margaret and Ciara are my life coaches. I owe them everything.

Finally, my deepest thanks to Coaches Paul Doherty, Shaunard Harts, Derek Swafford, Michelle Massari, Greg Norris and Justin Gatling as well as educator Chris Orr. Your dedication to students is true heroism. Thank you.

About Maureen O'Leary Wanket

Maureen O'Leary Wanket is a writer and teacher living in Sacramento, California with her husband and two daughters. *How to Be Manly* was inspired by the humor and courage of the students she's met in her classrooms over the past twenty years. She loves high school football, but only when she happens to teach at least half of the players on the field.

Her short stories have appeared in *Esopus, Xenith, Fiction at Work, Blood and Thunder, Musings on the Art of Medicine* and *Prick of the Spindle*.

Maureen writes articles about issues in education for local and national publications. She also muses about inspirations for a writer's life at maureenoleary.wordpress.com.

How to Be Manly is Maureen's first published novel. Follow her writing and publishing adventures on Twitter @maureenow.

About Giant Squid Books

Giant Squid Books is a publishing community founded by readers to support writers. It is GSB's mission to publish, support, and promote debut authors of young adult fiction, and to help them navigate the world of online publishing. To learn more about GSB, visit www.giantsquidbooks.com and follow along on Twitter @GiantSquidBooks.